Tales from
The Sunlit Garden

J C Milne
with illustrations by
Juliet Barton and the author

Published in 2015 by FeedARead.com Publishing for Adela Books,
J Christie, 3 An Goirtean, Brevig, Isle of Barra, HS9 5UA

To Juliet,

With thanks

Author's Preface

When these stories were begun the eldest gardener (grand)child was a very small flower in the sunlit garden. At the time of printing she was ten years old. I hope that these tales will be enjoyed by children of ten and upwards – and by those who have not forgotten having once been a child of ten and upwards!

More gardener children came along to enjoy the sunlit garden. One of them always has stories and pictures in her head. There is an earnest and methodical boy child, and at the time of writing there are two more little gardener children, who love to climb and play. You may find them in the stories.

The sunlit garden is real, but I have lent it my imagination. Don't come looking for it; let it stay in yours.

JCM.

Contents   Page

1. The Hoppity Flower

In her morning garden the gardener had made a patio. She made it using cool grey slate from the quarries of Ballachulish, far away on the other side of the sparkling sea.

On the cool grey slate a shaft of golden sunlight fell.

"Wake up!" cried the sun as it made the sea jump with light. "Can't you see me climbing high over the headland that protects you from the cold winds of the night? Wake up and talk to me!"

On the patio in the morning garden there stood resplendent two large, green garden tubs, whose inhabitants were all still fast asleep, and one tub that used to be a supreme shade of red, but which had spent much too long sun-bathing, and which had now turned a very tired-looking brown.

In the brown pot clustered some young green leaves, thick and strong. They hoped one day to cherish amongst them the exotic orange blooms of the summer lily.

But in the very centre of the lily leaves there had also grown a tall, slim stem. At the top of the stem was a bright yellow flower, which the sun had just woken up.

"You down there!" boomed the sun, when it caught sight of the tiny golden petals glistening, "What are you doing wearing my very own cloth of gold? What is your name?"

The golden flower shook a little at the blustering tone of the great giant of the sky.

"I don't know if I have a name, "she whispered. "You see," she bent her head slightly to peep at the neat patio, the dew-strewn lawn, and the fresh green of all the thirsty leaves, "I'm the only one. There are no others like me in the garden."

"Ho, ho, ho!" roared the sun, so that she thought he would fall out of the sky with laughing. "Only one of you, eh? Soon, as long as I keep shining, there will be a million like you! Two million, perhaps!"

"Not if we have anything to do with it," came a low grumble from the heart of the brown pot.

"Pardon?" murmured the flower, in some trepidation.

"You heard!" And the lily leaves waved crossly. "Just because we are leaves, and not flowers, doesn't mean we don't have a voice in the world. We know our duty! We are to here to protect the delicate Lady Lily, whom the likes of you can only gaze at. That is why the gardener takes special care of us. Now, you, you're in the way, and shouldn't be in our lily pot at all. You're nothing but a weed! Out you go! Hop it! Hop it! Hop it!"

And the leaves of the unborn lily, whose voice was still unheard, closed round the stem of the golden flower, until she heard the sickening crunch of stalk that told her she was cut through, and must now die. Then the leaves released her, and a small beneficent breeze lifted her gently over the edge of the pot, and carried her down. She lay in the trickle of grass beside the patio, grateful for its shelter. The high walls of her former home cast a shadow now that engulfed her in its black depths. The sun, impatient and bursting with life, had already moved higher, knowing nothing of the fate of the flower that wore his very own cloth of gold.

"Well, I am alive still," said she, "and I have a name now. 'Hop it', said the leaves. So I am The Hoppity Flower."

She lay in the shade of the pot and thanks to its coolness she did not yet die. She looked up at the heavens and watched a white cloud making a path across the sky. She thought that she with her thousand golden petals would soon rise to heaven, and colour the cloud gold. She saw herself as a bright angel face shining down on the garden, and felt a moment's happiness.

Crash! Thunder! Roar! What was this new horror?

It was a scary brown monster!

It bellowed and burrowed its way across the trembling grass, and in its wake lay devastation. The flower watched in alarm as the machine battered its way up and down, up and down the garden, while the shorn grass shrieked under its menacing blades. Even the lily leaves stirred their tips and deigned to remark upon the plight of those lesser beings that lived outside the brown pot. But The Hoppity Flower could tell that they had little sympathy for anyone else but themselves, and she wished that their Lady Lily might bring them joy.

She had no time to consider that she herself would never see the great flower, because at that very moment she knew that she was caught up in the blades of the fearsome cutting machine. She breathed a great gasp of the sweet garden air, and prepared to die. Yet, strangely, she found that she had not been hurt. By luck she had slipped through the jaws of death, into the damp quiet of the box where the pile of shorn grass grew denser by the minute, and where she was very nearly smothered, until she lifted her head clear.

"Life is very strange," thought The Hoppity Flower, "short, and full of surprises."

It was a little later, when, cushioned by the mown grass, she lay in the corner of the garden, that the gardener child found her.

"Oh, a lovely flower!" and she was caught up in a human hand; eyes as blue and wide as the sky endowed her with instant love. She tried to smile at the child who had rescued her, but she was too weak and limp to move her head.

Her new home was even stranger than before, and more elevated than the lily pot. She was placed in her own glass, and given life-prolonging water; and placed on the windowsill of the gardener's house, from where she could look down on the two green garden tubs and the old brown pot.

9

They are not as grand as they thought themselves; their pot is not as fine as the others, nor even as pretty as my glass," she thought. "But they are right – if I had not become The Hoppity Flower and hopped to the ground I would have taken the Lady Lily's place, and that would not do."

"I found a dandelion!" said the child, standing back to admire her.

"*Dents de lion*," said the gardener. "Lion's Teeth! It is sometimes called, 'Sun's Rays' as well."

She had not one, but two, names! "Lion's Teeth"! She was glad she had found it out, though it was a most peculiar name to have. It sounded brave, not at all like her. And "Sun's Rays"! How fine that sounded, though she had seen the sun in the sky and knew that he was far away indeed.

She knew that she would not last much longer, without her roots. The next time the sun came up he did not speak to her, or even see her, behind her walls of glass. She wondered if it was because she had lost his very own cloth of gold. She was no longer bright yellow, but pale and quite threadbare. She felt old, and feeble, and thought she must be nearly as light as air.

The next day the child cried out when she saw her whitened, feathery head. She lifted her gently from the glass, and took her to the open door of the house. The Hoppity Flower could just see the morning garden in all its glory – and, yes, there was the brown tub in which she had begun her life. She peered across, as well as she could; the lily leaves were looking a little tired, she thought, and, sure enough, there was the first wonderful bud of the flower they hosted, the Lady Lily who would in turn sap their strength. She almost thought she could catch sight of a glimpse of gold, orange-gold, darker than the sun whose colour she used to wear.

The Hoppity Flower was lifted up to the sun, and felt on her the lightness of the child's breath as she blew her feathery seeds, counting, "one o'clock, two o'clock, three o'clock, four ..." . The seeds rose in the air and scattered in the breeze, and it did seem, at that last moment of her life, as if she heard the bright sun laughing,

"Ho, ho, ho! A million of you! Two million, perhaps!"

2. La Reine des Prés
(*The Queen of the Meadows*)

Everyone in the garden was very excited. The sturdy, bright marigolds, orange and yellow, could talk about nothing else; even the gentle sweet peas whispered softly to each other and trembled in every breeze.

The Queen was coming. It was time for her annual visit. Of course, she never came quite into the garden, for really she was queen of the meadows, and the long feathery grasses there were her courtiers. She took up her summer residence just outside the pinewood fence in the north garden. On this particular morning the north garden was golden with early sunlight. The sparkling sea threw glittering light over it, for there was no hedge between them, just an uneven path of slate and brick, and a slatted gate. The tall iris leaves, the *sealeastair*, practised their greeting as they waved in a fresh little wind, and the willow tree bent right over the fence to get a closer view of the coming of the queen. The gardener had made all ready. The grass in front of the fence had been shorn especially by the clever son, so that everyone who lived nearby might enjoy the courtly display.

Of course, there were some, in the upper reaches of the south garden, who would not see, no matter how much they craned their necks and bent and waved. They tried not to be too disappointed. They were new this year to the garden, tall yellow flowers still without names, and they had their own pleasures; due to the wind that during the winters laid their surroundings bare, they could look always at the sparkling sea.

For some time now the slender stem of the queen of the meadows had been preparing itself. It had produced decorative, dusky green leaves set decorously in threes, at intervals up the red stem. This was an idea borrowed from an artist long ago who wandered the far fields. For a short while she had made her home nearby, in the flat, magical landscape of Heth, the land below the waves, and she had come on a short visit. When the artist made her dinner she created it as if it were a picture. She made a plateful of colours, green, red, and, to crown it all, white. For instance she might prepare young, fresh green dandelion leaves with red radishes and then add creamy white onion bulbs (she always knew where to find these things and so lived very happily on a palate of green, red and white). She was fond of the words *palate*, *palette* and *plate*, and played about with them. She spoke them to the world, and wished it, "Bon Appétit!" The stem of the meadow queen would blush with pleasure at the memory of the artist of the far fields and so had turned a delicate reddish hue.

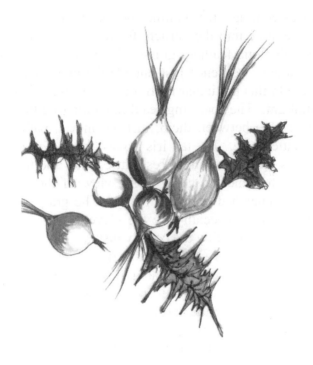

When the queen came she was white, a creamy, warm, summery white, not at all aloof or strange. Everyone loved her at once. She was announced by a fanfare of bees, and bowed her head to the dance of the iris. One large iris flower, which was just about to burst open, held her bud tightly shut so as not to intrude upon the sustenance of the white. The spell of the white was like snow on a sunlit mountain. Everyone longed to be there, to be part of it, to keep it for ever. They knew they could not, because the best things in life are only put there for a little while, but if you are lucky they come back year after year, because they too share a little part of you. They have borrowed your admiration.

The queen of the meadows had the gentlest nature in the world; perhaps this was because, from her tall red stem, she could see all of the world. From her compassionate heart sprung countless tiny petals of light and summer snow. They were a healing presence, amongst the harsh yellow of the iris and the spiky ladder of the quarrelsome thistle.

The summer went on. The sun, giant of the sky, was glad to be able to spend some time in his north garden. Sometimes, when the earth turned away from him in the winter months, he could not reach so far round. For this reason there were few flowers. Every morning the gardener opened the winter door and looked at the queen of the meadows outside the fence and wondered if that was why she, with her kind nature, had chosen the edge of the north garden for her summer palace.

Then one evening, when the gardener had restrained the boisterous Escallonia, which was always too big for its roots, and had gone tiredly indoors, the queen had a visitor. It was a calm evening, still full of light, and the midges were having another of their endless parties – fortunately these were silent affairs and did not impinge too raucously upon the evening peace. In its course, the moon rose, at first yellow over the bay, and with a smile threw a golden ladder over the sparkling sea. Then, when the sun had quite gone, right to the other side of the world, the moon turned silver and the ladder on the water jumped for joy, for here was the magic time.

And The Silver Witch came.

She was tall and wore black skirts, which only just trailed the earth. Her hair was black also, a little ragged round the edges, as if sometimes she cut off a lock of it for secret reasons of her own. She had compelling blue eyes, and a red mouth that sang strange spells to the garden. From her ears hung long blue and silver bells that looked like the earth itself as it spun round on its axis, and the flowers understood that even though they had closed their petals and were dreaming, she could hear their dreams. They shivered slightly, but the shivers were of excitement and anticipation, not fear. They knew The Silver Witch was good, because she understood them in their secret core.

She sometimes sang strange spells to the garden; but this night she had no words for them. She went straight to the queen of the meadows and had a long discourse with her. Every now and then the moon would shine brightly on them, and as the queen nodded her fair head it was possible to see that her beautiful crown was becoming indistinct, as if her petals were merging into each other, becoming a hazy floss of seed. Her puissant white had turned to a full and generous cream.

As the moon gazed down The Silver Witch stretched out her arm. Her long thin hand emerged from the folds of her violet-black garment. Her skin gleamed white, whiter now than the flowers of the queen. The nails of her spindly fingers were dusky green, like the leaves that curled before her. The garden flowers peeked from their closed petals and gasped. Their queen smiled on them for the last time, and was plucked.

The witch had already made her spell, and left it there, on the step for the gardener to find, along with the creamy down of the queen.

16

When morning came, the gardener looked out, as usual, from the north door, to greet the garden queen. But at her feet lay the plucked floss of the crown, and The Silver Witch's spell written on a large dock leaf.

The gardener took her presents into the house, and thought about them. In a cool, dim bedroom lay the gardener child, who loved the flowers. Her head ached, and her tummy was sore.

The gardener read the witch's leaf, made a special drink from the queen's flowers and gave it to the child, who smiled.

"It's sweet!" she said, and, after a little while, "I feel better now."

The gardener laid the remaining flowers beside her.

"These are a gift from La Reine des Prés," she said, "The Queen of the Meadows".

"I know a better name", said the gardener child, "I shall call her 'Meadow Sweet' because she is kind, and her flowers taste good."

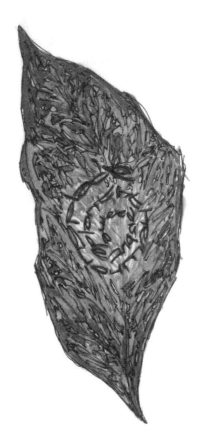

3. War

"Don't touch!" said the gardener to her child. "This plant is very dangerous!"

The gardener child looked in alarm at the stalky white plants outside the south fence. The south fence was not in good repair. It was attacked periodically by sheep and even the odd horse. When the horse had come the fence had been laden with electrical bolts, until the gardener had fought for its impunity.

"This is a garden," she had said to the invading human who trailed wires and giant pincers behind him, "not a prison camp." And she had indicated the child at her side, and the man had gone.

The south garden was a beleaguered place. You have already heard of the winds that lashed it from round the great headland. You may imagine the murderous flocks of sheep that sometimes hurled themselves against the south garden, baaing and pushing to get in, to graze and gobble its bold grass before advancing on the luscious and delicate flowers of the lower reaches. One winter, made resolute by hunger, they had succeeded in jumping in, one by one, over the sagging fence-wire and past the half-rotted posts. In that place the gardener had propped up an old door, which had become a magical world for hundreds of tiny insects. You could see them if you looked in behind the door. The door, though, was not quite in the south garden, but in the windy gap between it and the north garden.

So the south garden was largely unprotected. When the horse had neighed goodbye (and that is another story) the willow and ash trees had sighed as the flighty Rosa Rugosa took the place where the horse used to stand, near their gentle branches. Rosa Rugosa was a free spirit. She was brave and adventurous, sprawling and thorny, with great pink and white flowers, sometimes growing together on the same bush. Every summer the gardener had to teach her the same lesson: "Keep your shoots to yourself. There isn't room for them all in here." Rosa Rugosa never listened, and flourished cheekily a few feet outside the south fence.

She was now the only protection they had.

The gardener child went to bed and dreamed of the dangerous plant. It was so terrifying that its name was used in old stories and poems to frighten people. I will tell you its name, so that you know never to touch it. It is called Hemlock. If, in a field or by the roadside, you see its tall, branching stem, with a lot of tiny white ball-like clusters at the top, don't touch it. I should say, don't touch *them*, because they will be legion.

You will not need to dream about them, because the gardener child has given me his dream, which is this.

The army was advancing. The tall yellow flowers right at the top of the south garden were the first to see it. They were so new and nameless that they didn't know it for the danger it was.

"How funny," they sang, "thousands of little umbrellas coming!"

Their neighbour the whitebeam tree usually tried not to listen to them, because they often talked nonsense. His attention was caught this time because he thought at first they were talking about him; then he remembered that his own harmless white flowers were quite gone already. The whitebeam tree was so ideally suited to the windy conditions of the south garden that he too has been put into poetry. Now the whitebeam tree was doing just what the poet George Meredith had written a long time ago: "flashing as in gusts the sudden-lighted whitebeam".

In other words, the tree got a fine fright when he saw the advancing army of hemlock. He was very old and knew well the danger that this menacing plant bore to the gardener children, if it ever got into the garden. He flashed his leaves white in the wind, and by this means warned the whole garden:

"Flak! Flak Attack! Enemy Invasion!"

The sparrows jumped up from their gossiping, and flew chirruping the news right round to the north garden, only stopping briefly to swoop down on the crumbs the gardener had put out for them on the patio. Snails stopped munching and raised their spindly horns to each other in disbelief; the smaller ones paled and retreated hurriedly into their shells. Yellowing leaves fluttered in panic from the sycamore tree, followed by hundreds of tiny winged seed pods sallying out to reconnoitre. Everyone in the garden joined in the general alarm.

What now to do? They had only a short time before the first of the plants crept through the south fence and got to the willow wood, where the weeping willows were now looking very depressed indeed. They bent and swayed, and sang mournful songs to each other. Grandfather Willow craned his neck to watch the advance, his top branches forking with the effort, and yes, there was the first hemlock, defiantly glaring at him from a small hillock. The first ground had been gained, the advantageous position taken. Grandfather Willow saw that the bulrushes had come to the aid of the garden, flanking the hemlock in the brown uniform of the defence corps, but there were too many paths through. The forces of the hemlock marched on, through the path of the nightmare, in threatening silence.

It was not a sociable plant.

In its path lay devastation. Its sweet cousin, the pretty yarrow, took the opportunity of flight. It carried its seeds, timorously, right to down to the verges of the shore road, where the sparkling sea gave it inspiration and succour. Even Old Giant Hogweed, general of the occupying forces, sat back and let the upstart hemlock take command. The poor blind earthworms shrank deep into their tunnels at its approach and the helpless earwigs scuttled. The marching ants, on whom the inhabitants of the field had thought to depend, had better causes to march for than this. They raked through the fallen sycamore leaves, which had given their lives in order to throw a rampart of yellow-brown over the entrance to the garden. The ants filed through these flimsy defences in their endless, dutiful scavenging, prising out any refugees who had taken cover in the leaves, wood-louse or mite.

Their heartlessness pervaded the child's dream of the hemlock, and he shivered as he lay in his dark room. The black panic of the cowering insects fluttered into the heart of the child, and the dark power of the hemlock reached even into the borders of the land of sleep.

In his dream the child got up, obeying a call greater than fear. He looked out of his window, and saw, with a feeling of dread and apprehension, the white hemlock forming a chain of might across the captured hillock. In the depths of the night the plants were dragon-like, grotesque. The flak-like heads of the cavalry were held high, silhouetted against a thin moon. The old brown seed-pods of the vanguard looked like a carapace of distorted, crackling bombs, set to burst upon the garden of delight he called his own.

Solemnly the child left his room and crept downstairs. He knew his moment had come, and he knew what he had to do. He walked firmly to the north garden, which was in no danger. He walked past the vigilant scrub willow, which was awake worrying about its relations in the south garden, and opened the door of the old shed.

The old shed was a most marvellous place. I shall not describe it here, because at night its dark, unidentifiable shapes, its peculiar, mothy smells, were almost as terrifying to the gardener child as the thought of the advancing hemlock; but he knew what he wanted, and went fearlessly through the crouching blades, the gleaming racks of toothy saws, and the bottles that he knew contained Poison.

Hanging above his head was sheaf upon sheaf of magical but benign herbs. There hung yarrow, clover, meadowsweet and eyebright, grown or gathered by the gardener herself, ruler of the garden. In the dream he was tall, and reached them easily. He carried a spade as if it were light as a feather. He returned for a tall pile of empty garden pots. He took them all to the door at Windy Gap, which had now turned into a refugee camp for fleeing insects, and laid them down. He thrust the door aside with all his strength. Beetles, spiders and all manner of grubs emitted a kind of collective scream as they were uncovered, their new refuge destroyed. With the strength of the hero he pitied their plight but knew he had needed to take what they had. They were part of the casualties of war.

Now it was easy for him to reach the wide outdoors. But the dream of the hemlock was strong. The nearer he got to the enemy, the more its magical powers slowed him down. He persevered. The dream, the nightmare, lasted, it seemed, for ever. With the huge, heavy spade he dug and built defences, piling stones into a long trench all along the outside of the south fence. He knew that the hemlock was gaining on him.

He took his bunches of yarrow, clover, meadowsweet and eyebright, and his pots. He knew the herbs were magic, and he saw that they needed now to become concentrated, thick and warlike. He invoked the pretty yarrow, cousin of the dreaded hemlock, with its power to lull, soothe and numb. Carefully, with the slowness of dream, he filled each of his pots. He gathered the moisture of the night dew in his hands, and pushed the herbs down, packing them hard into the pots. He lined them up, in front of the trench of stones he had built, in a wall of defence that was also a secret weapon.

It was all taking too long. He would never finish in time. He heard the low moan of the whitebeam tree, which was keeping guard, and knew that he was only a small boy before a numberless force. But, just as the slowness of the dream began to overpower him, there rose in the air a strange laughter, and he looked up. In the pale moon it seemed to him that a lady stood there, green and red, large and abundant. She laughed with glee, and flashed him a thousand pinpricks of light; they were her thorns, and she was the Lady Rosa Rugosa.

He heard the hemlock soldiers wince with pain as their smooth, unlined stems met the barbed defence of the rose. She had tightened her grip; the shoots to whom the gardener had denied entrance had clustered thick and strong, and these last days had been consolidating their own army. They rose up now in a solid wall of thorn and bush; the enemy was temporarily stayed. The willow trees in the south garden nodded their gratitude, and the child felt that their thanks were for him also, as he continued to build what had now become the rear defences.

Finally his sharp-stoned trench, with its barricade of pots, was ready.

The Rosa Rugosa, looking now rather more like a bush than a lady, seemed to nod her approval, and her leaves rustled with the tiniest murmur of inquisitiveness. He was cold now, and very tired, but he turned each pot over, just as if he was making a sandcastle. He tapped each one sharply with the flat of his spade, and out came a castle of herbs. He set them out in a row, so that they made a great turret of rebuttal. If the hemlock tried to get past them, their scent would send them to sleep, and into the trench they would fall.

The Rosa Rugosa gave a great yawn, and the willows sobbed with relief. The defences would stand. The gardener child walked back into his house and up to his room. From his window he looked down already into a dense flock of white. The flat heads of hemlock, which sent to innocent victims the sleep of death, had now themselves become victims, lulled and felled so that they lined his trench with their dying. They were the vanquished now, and he could sleep.

When morning came he went at once to the window, the conqueror surveying the battle spent. But what was this? How was the field still full of the vicious plant? What had happened to his strategy, his defence? Waking slow from the bonds of the night, he went outside in his pyjamas and found the gardener already at work. She was standing at Windy Gap, propping up again the old door, which had fallen over.

"It must have been very windy last night," she said, "For this old door to be on the ground."

She saw that the child was bewildered, and did not mention the disorder in which she had just found her garden shed. He has been digging out the ground for the new fence, she thought, and has not put

24

the spade away.   But I must hang the herbs higher up in future; somehow he has knocked them down.

They stood together, and the boy rubbed his eyes.   The early morning light was hazy, but the white sun was already climbing.   Over the hemlock field there was a barely perceptible movement, as of millions of tiny wings, a bright, scintillating murmur in the air.

"Look!" said the gardener.   The silver ground moth has come on the wind.   It will eat up all those hemlock plants that have nearly come into the garden.   Then we will be safe."

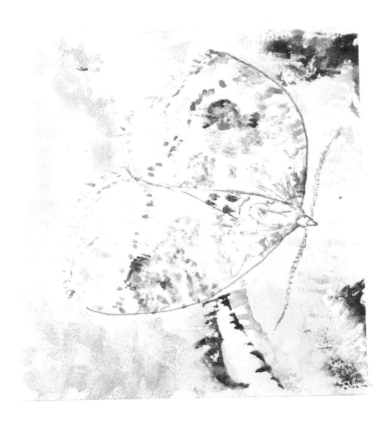

4. A Tale of Colours

"We are a late flowering," explained the low-growing, dark green plant newly in front of the fuchsia. It was in conversation with the female blackbird, for whom this was a favourite part of the garden. She would come every morning to the washing basket stone on the triangle of short-cropped grass under the washing lines. The female blackbird came to watch the song thrush at work. The song thrush believed in killing two birds with one stone, as the saying goes, or at least killing one snail by tapping its shell against the stone while at the same time waking up the gardener, who liked to sleep with the bedroom window open. The female blackbird would wait until the thrush had cracked open the snail, then, swipe! Off she would fly with the soft snail, for her children, of course, not for herself, no, no.

This particular morning was wet and autumnal. The path glittered and shone. The particular snail the thrush had selected for her breakfast was old and fat with a thick, hard shell.

It was just the sort of morning the snail liked. He had already been on a jaunt in the old southernwood bush and had just been strolling along to the lesser chives when the thrush spotted him and began tap-tapping away with him on the stone. The snail began to feel somewhat light-headed and anxious. The female blackbird, waiting in the wings, out of boredom and frivolousness asked the low-growing dark-green plants nearby if they couldn't make up their minds as to which colour their flowers were supposed to be.

The dark-green plants conferred with each other, and the foremost one deigned to answer.

"We are a late flowering," said he, "because we have many colours to build and produce. Ours is an old story, which is long to tell and even longer to listen to."

The female blackbird cocked her ear attentively while the thrush tap-tapped the snail. She had plenty of time.

"You will notice," began the plant in declamatory style, that my purple is deeper than that of the heather on the hillside, and the white of this plant behind me has the dazzling clarity of the autumn sun; and that the red of my neighbour here is redder than blood."

"Blood?" said the female blackbird nervously. She had once seen blood, on a shrew that the cat had left on her stone. It had dried brown like her feathers, and it stank of death. Like all females, she knew her own mind, and had decided long ago that her plumage was to be brown, not black like her husband's, no matter what name she was known by. But did this red stuff lie beneath her brown feathers? She looked at the thrush still tap-tapping the snail. Did even snails bleed?

27

"Our colours," continued the plant, "are the colours of the hill and shore, meadow and moor. They dyed the cloth the humans wore who walked this land. They took the bark of the oak – he indicated the sad oak, who lived in worry because he had heard the gardener say once that he had been planted too near the house, and must one day be cut down – and they chose also the hawthorn and the alder, for their black, of strength and sorrow. The elderberry there" - he inclined himself, in order to see the yellow elderberry bush at Windy Gap – "well, not that particular one, because it bears only blossom" (at this the ill-favoured bush looked down, and tried to hide itself) – "and the wild blaeberries of the hillside gave them the blue of melancholy. For the reds, purples, browns and yellows of turning hopes they scoured the lichens of the shore, as well as certain plants not represented here within my (admittedly rather limited) field of vision. Even the terrible ugly ragwort had its use, producing a rather garish orange that in my opinion should be used only very discreetly. You will notice *our* blooms have not this shade."

Some of the plants behind him coughed rather pointedly, to remind him to get on with the story. They knew that this tale could be as long as the hills were high and the sea wide.

"Yes, that was how the humans dressed then," said a new voice. It was the snail, who had poked its head out. The thrush had caught sight of a cat and flown a little way away. "I know it because the molluscs on the shore told me. They know many ancient stories."

He caught a flash of the blackbird's eye, which had lit upon him in surprise, and ducked back into his shell again before the bright beak pounced. The blackbird gave him a couple of desultory taps, to remind him she knew he was in there.

"Yes," continued the speaker plant, to no one in particular, "They dressed in the colours of the earth and sea. This was how they knew themselves.'

'They would choose different colours and patterns according to the family to whom they belonged, just as we plants do. They called these 'tartans', which sounds strange in the English tongue, but in their language was simply *tarsuinn*, meaning that the cloth they wove was wrapped across their bodies in a plaid. They were proud to wear their colours, just as we love to show off our distinctive blooms. Look at

Madam Purple there – she is edged all in white, as if the daisies were paying her court!"

The female blackbird looked at her brown feathers. She was not bright like the flowers. But she wondered why she had allowed her husband to choose the black of strength and sorrow, for didn't they belong to her too?

"But to my tale," continued the flower, in his dreamy fashion, "The humans brought their colours to battle, to fight for the land they walked and the king who had ruled over them. He was youthful, and bonny as a flower, and they would have no truck with the foreign king who wished to conquer their land. When the bright regiments stood there, on Culloden Moor, how like flowers they seemed!"

Here the plant paused, and bowed his leaves, respectfully. The female blackbird thought of all the many things she had to do that morning. There was such a nice clump of dug earth waiting for her, where she knew the juicy worms would be cavorting . . .

The plant's changed tone called her back from her pleasant reverie.

"They were plucked, trampled, destroyed. The man of black who did this is known, in these parts, as The Butcher."

The blackbird, slightly embarrassed by the new turn the story had taken, remembered the snail, who was now attempting to crawl away before the thrush came back. With a quick hop she was there in front of him.

"Stinking Billy"! He cried, before withdrawing into his shell again.

"That is right," nodded the plant. That is what he was, and it is written in books that that name is sometimes given to us, because our colours are the colours he trampled with his boots and swords. But it is not true! It is the bold ragwort that has this name, and deservedly so, for it destroys all others.'

'This Butcher not only killed the human flowers but banned the wearing of their colours for ever, because the *tarsuinn* showed the humans who they were. No more would the colours of earth and shore be woven into human souls. In their hearts the music of colour was stilled, and the music of their pipes too fell away, banned with the colours they wore when they played.'

'This man, I say, was known in these parts as The Butcher. But," and here all the dark-green plants sighed in unison, because they knew what was coming next, "his real name was William of Marlborough, Duke of Cumberland." The speaker plant hung his head. "His

29

victorious people gave us his name, and called us also sweet, because they rejoiced as the Flower of Scotland was trodden down."

There was silence after the flower's story. The female blackbird had hopped down to the lesser chives. There were usually fat little grubs there to be gobbled up. She thought of her children, grown up now and flown away. Where had they gone, and where they were, were there fat grubs to be enjoyed?

"Excuse me," came the voice of the snail again, emboldened now since the thrush had flown off and the blackbird's attention was elsewhere, "These old plants beside you, sir, have given up producing flowers. I have not seen any from them this season or last. But you, who have arrived recently, perhaps from the very field of Culloden itself, *qui le sait*, who knows? – You are bearing their bright colours again. It doesn't matter what they call you. Sticks and stones, you know . . ." and remembering the washing basket stone where perhaps his own fate awaited, he set off at a rapid pace (for a snail) right under the fuchsia bush, out of the way of predatory beaks.

The resplendent fuchsia, with its flowers that hung blood-red, smiled down at the Sweet William.

"Don't be ashamed, little plant," she said. "I have heard a different story. It is that the true meaning of your "William" is "oeillet", Little Eye, who sees and knows what is true. Look at me! I have many varieties and many names. Every year they cut me down, and my flowers weep blood. But every year I come back, proud and strong and glorious, just like you."

5. The Oak Tree

The oak tree, as you may have heard, lived in worry, because he had heard his life was to be shortened. He was young and lithe, and could not understand why the gardener had said that one day he would be cut down.

He was older than the gardener children, that was certainly true. He spent his days looking in at them as they played in their house made of wood. The timber for their house came from a faraway land called Scandinavia, beyond the sparkling sea, but he had, he felt, a sort of kinship with it, as it had once been a tree like him. The wooden house had big bay windows that looked out onto the south garden, at the bottom of which the oak tree lived.

"That's the problem," the gardener had explained one day to her friend, the man who watched the distant hills. It was planted too near the house. One day its roots will be too big for the foundations. It will have to be cut down, I expect, but maybe not in our lifetime".

"In *my* lifetime, though!" the tree had thought in alarm, and had never quite recovered since.

It was always last to come into leaf in the spring, for it did not want to grow too big and be noticed. Luckily for it, the gardener did not often look at its height. She would look down, at the soft earth at the foot of the tree, for there was buried a tiny human, a gardener child that had never played, with the others, in the wooden house.

So the oak tree had grown, but had still not produced any acorns. It kept itself to itself, and was somewhat blighted.

This day was to be a day of storm. The trees all knew it, and had become a little frantic, especially Grandfather Willow, who was always the first to come into leaf in the spring, for he loved to show off

31

his fresh yellowy-green foliage against the deep blue of the spring sky; but he knew also that his fickle leaves were quick to desert him when the winds of autumn came. He was the first of the trees to be stripped bare. Then the wounds in the pink skin of his trunk would be revealed, where the gardener had cut his low-growing branches so that he could not catch and hinder her washing as it blew on the line, which he loved to do.

Grandfather Willow did not allow this to bother him at all. He was excited by the thought of the coming gale. The oak tree could hear him laughing as his leaves flew off and blew all over the south garden. Then the tall French windows of the wooden house burst open, and out sailed the littlest gardener child with her ball, straight into the arms of the tree.

"It tickles! Ooh, it tickles!" laughed Grandfather Willow, as the brightly-coloured ball bounced up into his branches, again and again, blue and red and yellow all at once, spinning in the wind. Sometimes he would manage to hold on to it for an instant in his spindly grasp, and then he and the child would laugh all the more heartily as the ball would run along the branch, tip off onto the next one and down to the ground, to be caught once more and flung high again into the air.

The oak tree gave a little smile. He wondered what it felt like to have such fun. He only knew fun as he saw it sometimes through the windows of the wooden house.

The autumn sun threw golden rays over the pink-hued trunk of the willow, picking out with shadow the dents and ravages of its bark. On the oak tree it lit delicately the gentle green of the outer leaves. The oak tree would hang onto its leaves beyond the passing of all the others, because they clothed him in a kind of ease; they hid and protected him. It may have been that the sun, giant of the sky, loved him especially, and shone on him late into the autumn.

The oak tree could hear the child now up at the top of the south garden with her ball. In the open heights, where pine trees had once tried to live and had been turned brown and killed by south-easterly gales, the child and the ball played on the grass.

"This is just the right place to be with my ball," was the arabesque that the child danced. She did not put this dance into words, because she was still a little young for the limitations of words, and knew only the freedom of being.

Soon the ball leapt down the stone step into the middle garden, where the spreading hazel grew. The child sat on her bottom and scrambled down after it. The hazel tree kindly put out her lower branches, to stop the child going from the sunlit garden to the outer edge, and the child stood uncertainly, looking for her ball. The oak tree saw that it had run with the wind into the dense path to the east, under the nameless trees. They huddled together, darkly, looking rather severely at the ball, an intruder, round and quite obviously rootless.

"He is not like us," they said. "He has no roots or branches. Why is he here?"

The ball said nothing, as it was really only a piece of plastic cleverly wrapped around air. Perhaps it was the air inside it that gave it its semblance of life. Or perhaps it needed the gardener child in order to come alive. In the tunnel under the nameless trees, there was no child and no wind to move it.

"What shall we do with it?" the nameless trees asked each other. "It can't stay here. It is quite out of place here."

"And what if," hissed the white convulvus, which lived by winding itself round the trees and sucking the life out of them, without their knowing, "what if it tries to put down roots here?"

"Heaven forbid!" cried the trees in horror, and begged the wind to take it away again. The convulvus was pleased. She did not welcome intruders. She worked herself round the nameless trees, softly strangling them to death, so very softly that they did not notice until it was too late.

The oak tree watched the child standing under his neighbour the spreading hazel. The child stepped across the narrow path between the middle garden and the window lawn, which was his. He bent down as far as he could and gave her his soft leaves to play with. The sun, giant of the sky, noticed and shone harder, so that the child sank down in the warm grass and kissed it. The she put her arms around the oak tree, and kissed it too.

"This is better than fun," whispered the oak tree to himself, "this is comfort, and this is sustenance. This is what I can give."

Why did the wind blow just then with more strength, so that even the warmth of the sun, giant of the sky, was dimmed? Grandfather Willow shrugged his shoulders, and the kind hazel felt sad for the oak that his moment was so short. The wind rustled the leaves on the oak tree, and the little one looked up. A gate banged in the morning garden, and round the corner came The Visitor Dog.

The Visitor Dog was large and black, with a big red mouth. He was the happiest dog in the world, because he did not know anything. The gardener child squealed as he licked her all over and knocked her over in his joy, back down under the oak tree. Then he bounded away, right into the dense path, where he had caught sight of the bright ball. In a moment he was back out, throwing and catching the ball with his great mouth. The child laughed with pleasure.

"Don't let the dog. . ." came the voice of the gardener as she opened the French windows; but it was too late, for the sharp white teeth of The Visitor Dog had broken through the ball. The air rushed out and the ball stuck out, flattened, from the animal's jaws.

The child sobbed, and the gardener took the ball from the dog, who stood wagging his tail in mute apology.

"It's not his fault," she said, "That's what dogs do. I will buy you a new ball."

"It won't be my happy ball," said the child in her wordless way, but the oak tree understood, and was grieved for someone else, and not for himself.

35

"Ball dead now," said the child, in words. The gardener gave her the flattened piece of plastic, so that she could look once more at its bright pattern.

The gardener child placed the ball carefully under the oak tree, where life that was ended lay, and the gardener nodded.

They walked together into the house, before the great gale came and in its bluster carried off the flat piece of plastic. The sparkling sea had by this time become slate grey; but in the tiny spot where the dead ball fell the fierce waves gleamed with a sudden flash of rainbow light.

6. The Horse Who Said Goodbye

The gardener, though to the garden omnipotent, was only a gardener. About horses she was an ignoramus, which means she knew nothing, or very little, only that horses were large and ate her garden.

Actually she had never thought about horses eating her garden until one did. The horse arrived one damp spring morning in the field outside the south garden and straight away stuck its head over the fence for a tasty breakfast of The Lady Fuchsia's delicate, succulent leaves, arranged so conveniently in close-growing clusters. How the horse enjoyed that first good chomp! He whinnied in delight.

The gardener was out, in the world beyond the garden. When she came back, through the swinging gate, she cast her eye over everything, as usual, for all signs of growing green, and then took her shopping into the wooden house. The plants waited rather nervously. Everyone had heard about the new arrival, and the neglected trees in the evening garden had been able to watch the whole show. First the large red horse box had been parked at the far side of the next-door field, and then the great horse had clopped out. Within a minute the news was all round the garden, carried First Class, by the chirpy messenger sparrows.

After a good trot round the field, the horse, as we have said, had found the fuchsia. Eventually it had gone back to the other side of the field, nibbling the grass as it went; but that did not stop the dazzling white bluebells in the morning garden wishing they could be among

37

their cousins in the south garden so they could watch what happened next. The white bluebells were called 'Erratic', which means they had come from who knows where, and were not proper bluebells at all. Experts said they did not grow at all in the gardener's island. The gardener thought they might be a hybrid. A hybrid means a mix of things. The white bluebells didn't concern themselves and just got on with looking dazzling.

The French windows opened and the gardener stepped out with the washing. The next moment she dumped the washing basket onto the ground and ran across to her nibbled fuchsia. In the spring-bare garden it was easy for all the growing things to watch her as she discovered with amazement the new resident of the next-door field. The horse saw her too and innocently started to come towards her. Perhaps he was hoping for a juicy carrot, or just wanted to say hello.

But the gardener ran back inside the wooden house, and the trees and the sparrows listened to a voice they had never heard their gardener use before, a voice that grew crosser and harder by the minute. It was exciting, though! They wondered what would happen next, after the gardener had finished speaking very loudly into her telephone. But nothing did, except that she came out every now and then, glared at the horse and shouted at it to go away. The horse, slightly alarmed, would retreat a few yards and gradually work his way back, munching the fresh grass as he came.

The whole of the south garden came to like the horse. He would often come to the old fence, not just to chew the fuchsia when the gardener wasn't looking, but because he liked company. He knew that the fence, the house, the washing line, and the children's slide, meant people, with their attractions of warmth, food and care. The horse liked all these things. No one had ever explained to him that he was not supposed to join in. He had no other horse to keep him company. Grandfather Willow, whose domain was the south garden fence, allowed his new young buds and leaves to brush the horse's long nose as he looked over the fence, and sometimes he tickled him with his soft young shoots.

"Neigh!" answered the horse, who at heart was a simple soul, and he threw his head up in pleasure, opening his soft mouth and dilating his nostrils.

"You again!" screeched the gardener, leaping out of the wooden house. "Get away! Get away!" And this time the horse galloped off.

The garden went silent. The gardener poked rather sullenly around Grandfather Willow, to see what damage might have been done to him. He poked her in return with one of his pokier twigs, which got stuck in her hair.

The next time the gardener shooed off the horse, she brought a stick. She hit the fence with it hard, which might have broken the old fence, because it was very ramshackle and the horse was a lot gentler with it than the gardener had become. The horse kept further back now, but there were times, in the evening when the gardener had gone in, that he came quietly up to Grandfather Willow to hear his soft rustling and have the young willow twigs scratch his long nose. The fuchsia didn't mind him at all. She quite liked having her outside leaves nibbled by the horse and her stems stroked by his hairy sides. She knew that she could grow lots more leaves.

"You're getting too tall anyway," laughed the rowan beside her, "if it weren't for the horse I wouldn't be able to see over the top of you!"

"And I'd get a big draught round my roots," put in Grandfather Willow. "You're getting a bit woody down below, and the wind blows right through you. You let the horse chop off a bit of your heady growth, young lady, and fill out a bit so that you grow strong and thick. That's the way a fuchsia ought to be!"

The fuchsia felt the tickle of the horse enjoying her leaves for his supper and the company of the garden, and thought how lonely he must have been up on the hillside all winter, and how there were no delicious leaves for him to eat up there.

"We've finished with our leaves now!" sang out the white bluebells that had worked their way round to the bay windows. You can eat ours too!"

The horse gave his whinnying laugh.

"Thank you, little belles," he called, making what is known as a pun, that is that the flowers were bells and they were also *belle*, beautiful, "but you still need your leaves. You will produce more flowers next year if you keep them. And you are too near the house for me."

"Ride a cock horse, to Banbury Cross," sang the flowers gaily, "To see a fine lady upon a white horse. . . "

"With rings on her fingers and bells on her toes ..." neighed the horse, softly in case the gardener should hear him.

"She shall have music wherever she goes," finished the fuchsia, who rather wished that she was the lady in the song. And they had a fine party.

And so the summer came, and the horse did not eat the fuchsia now, because he had plenty of rich grass in the field. The gardener and he kept a wary eye on each other. She had developed a new fear, that he would jump right into the garden and gobble up all her best summer blooms. She knew that this was an irrational fear, which meant it had no basis in reality, and so she kept it carefully hidden. The gardener children loved the horse and would often call to him as they played their games in the sunlit garden. The horse did not always come, because he had learned to be careful, but if he happened to be near the fence, and one of them had an apple, he would take it from them gently, and let them stroke his nose.

Then a terrible apple disaster happened. Somehow the gardener had not realised why the children had suddenly become so fond of apples. One day she came out and saw the littlest gardener child feeding her apple to the horse. Her throat tightened with fear. She raced across, hearing the crack of the little one's thumb as the horse bit it off with its monstrous teeth - no! Thank goodness! It was only the cracking of the apple core. But the horse made off, startled, as she grabbed the child's hand, and the little one cried out in fright.

"If she had taught the child to keep its hand spread out," remarked Grandfather Willow grumpily to the garden at large, "or if she had been enjoying the horse's company with the child, there wouldn't have been a problem. I'm getting tired of all this."

Everyone in the garden was affected by the new aggression. The worst of it all was that it was their own beloved gardener who was causing it. The summer blooms faded swiftly, and the trees swished their leaves sadly as the winds turned to autumn chill.

One day the cold north wind arrived to tell the garden it was time to start looking to the winter. The bulbs of the hybrid Hyacinthoides Massartiana (or white bluebells) dug themselves deeper in to the earth, and the littlest ones, which the female blackbird had uncovered in her pecking, tried to raise themselves higher, so that the gardener would see them and rescue them. The early north wind blew away again, but left in its place the raucous crows, who quarrelled in the evenings and flitted noisily amongst the trees, scaring off the horse whenever it approached. Its owner, the man on the other end of the gardener's telephone, sometimes came to feed it now, at the far end of the next-door field, and the garden began to lose sight of their erstwhile friend.

One fine morning the little oak tree, who lived near the bay windows, was enjoying his favourite piece of music, which the gardener was playing on her piano. He had heard her say once that the piece was named "Morning", which the oak tree felt was very appropriate. It was all very pleasant.

It was then that man on the other end of the telephone arrived with a clatter, from across the field, and began desecrating the poor south garden fence with his sharp clippers and his electric wire. It was most undignified for the fence, which had stood there a very long time despite never having been painted or repaired. The oak tree knew that this was the result of all the arguments of the summer, on the gardener's telephone. He tried his hardest to reach the bay window with his branches, to attract the attention of the gardener, but he could not reach. The white bluebells that had lived there in the spring had long departed, with not even an adieu, so they could be of no help at all. The gardener played on, and not even she could be cross in the company of such beautiful music. But what was to be done? The man stamped about, and the fence shrieked every time he wrenched it with his cruel tools.

It was the horse that solved matters. Surprised and nervous itself, it neighed vehemently, several times. At last the gardener heard, and flew out in a burst of rage.

You know the end of the story of the electric fence, because you have heard of it in another tale. The altercation was not pleasant, but in the end the man retreated, with all his tools. When he had gone the gardener sat on the washing basket stone and wondered why she had stopped the man from keeping the horse away. Of course, it had been for the gardener children; but she knew that, also, she had not wanted the horse to be hurt by his electric bolts. She thought about the horse, and what he had brought to the garden.

She looked up, and there he was, standing quietly near his friend, Grandfather Willow. The gardener got up and went into the wooden house. She came back with a carrot, and then she called the horse to her, "Cou-cou, cou-cou, cou-cou", which was a funny thing to say to a horse but then about horses she was an ignoramus.

The horse came to her, with his gentle manner. In the garden it was remembered forever as a magical moment.

The gardener broke off pieces of the carrot and fed them to the horse, rather hesitantly at first, because she had never done it before. She kept her hand outstretched and tried not to listen to the crack, crack, as the strong teeth bit through the carrot. The horse looked at her with his soft, intelligent eyes, and she thought he must have the most liquid eyes in the world. She wondered what he was thinking behind those eyes and inside that great head. She watched his delicate, prehensile lips picking the carrot pieces from her hand, and thought perhaps she had been unjust to the horse. Her fuchsia, in contrast to the rest of the garden, had done quite well this summer.

The garden relaxed. As winter drew on the gardener often fed the horse. Sometimes she brought him a bucket of water, if his owner did not come. She stroked his coat and brushed mud off his legs. She had come to like the horse.

Then one day he went away. The red horse box was parked once more at the far end of the next door field. At the time the horse was standing in the spot where the gardener had planted the Rosa Rugosa, to keep away any more large animals the owner of the field might choose to send.

The horse was slow to realise what was happening, but Grandfather Willow, always vigilant, had just time to warn him, as the man made his determined way across the field. The horse turned his great head and gave a low, whinnying farewell to the garden, in a tone of regret, which everyone understood.

The trees nodded and whispered back, "Goodbye, dear friend!", but Grandfather Willow spoke out, in the language of wisdom,

"You took only what you needed, Horse, and have left us with something better."

"What is that?" called the little oak, who was already sad.

"*She* has learned to be kind," said Grandfather Willow, "and not before time, mind you."

7. The Great Quarrel

It was the kind of blowy day when nothing in the north garden could stay there. The north garden was a place of few flowers. All that blossomed there was hard and black, like the big bins and the slidy slates and the coal.

The big bins were soon overturned, and the lumps of coal skittered about on the slates. Had there been any flowers there, they would have been whirled up into the sky, where they could have listened at close hand to the great quarrel between the sun, giant of the sky, and the harvest moon.

It was the time of the equinox. This means that the sun is at its highest, and rises right in the east, exactly where it should, and sets right in the west, exactly where it should. The sun, although he was a giant and very grown up, liked to play 'hide and seek' in the sky. He was especially good at this amongst the trees of the south garden, who loved him for the golden splashes of warmth he threw across their trunks, and the flickering light he scattered among their leaves. Today, on this special day, he decided he would not play but would stay bright, and high, and tell the world down below that he was king. It was like a birthday for him, really, but without the cake and the candles.

Now, that was a fine plan, except that this year it happened also to be the time of the harvest moon, the moon that is round and full at the equinox. She had been filling out her fleshy belly on green cheese (which everybody knows is up there somewhere, along with the cow that jumped over the moon and never did come back down). The harvest moon was ready to show herself in her full glory, just when the sun had had sucked in a few dead planets for breakfast and was getting ready to go on parade. The moon was normally a gentle person who did not argue much with the bigger and stronger sun. But the moon had a very bossy cousin. Shall I tell you this cousin's name straight away, or would you like to guess? If you want to guess, then let me tell you that he comes to visit her twice a day and sometimes brings presents too. He brings seaweed and driftwood; he even sometimes brings seals, or a little boat that has lost its oars. He is very drawn to the moon and needs her silver magic so that he can weave his own spell and call human beings to take to the sea in ships.

He was the tide, and he was very high and mighty, heading right in to shore as the moon peeked out in her best silver dress, and throwing up his waves as if he were an orchestra clashing out a dramatic overture.

The tide was very cross that the sun always eclipsed the moon (which means that the moon could not be seen because of the sun's brighter light). They had had quarrels over this before, and, very occasionally, the moon would manage to get right in front of the sun so that she blocked him completely. Generally this only lasted a fraction of a second before the sun pushed her out of the way again.

"They're at it again," sighed the blackcurrant bush in the morning garden, which was the first place to witness the arrival of the tide, and the moon, and the fading of the twilight that announced the sun. "Fight, fight, fight! You'd think they'd just leave well alone."

"For once I agree with you," poked in the ubiquitous bramble. "If that gardener of yours had left well alone I'd still be living in my corner of the morning garden, there, beside that pathetic-looking redcurrant, instead of being pushed out here behind the fence."

"It's not my fault," answered the blackcurrant, crossly, "if she prefers me to you. At least I don't cut her hands all over when she picks *my* fruit."

The bramble thrust a particularly long and vicious-looking branch over the fence.

"Watch it or I'll give you a taste of my thorns! Where's your gardener friend to protect you now, eh?"

But the gardener, who was normally still in bed at this time, was standing nearby, which the blackcurrant bush was relieved to see. She looked over at the bramble just as if she had heard him. He cowered down, in the space she had left him between the fence and the next door shed, but he made sure he left a trailing branch out to scratch her legs if she came any nearer. The bramble was a bit like that, and for that reason the blackberries he gave were not very sweet. This was the real reason why he had been banned from the garden, although he was called "Fantasia", which had made the gardener believe he would produce a wonderful banquet.

The gardener had got up very early in order to see the harvest moon, which she loved. But the sky was strangely clouded, as if something was going on up there. Even as she watched, black rain clouds gathered, as if the dark seas had called them up in a spell, to give them back their water and their power, their movement and spite over the little earth. The soft twilight receded, but the sun did not come out to play, and the sky lightened not to blue, but to dark, awful purple.

The gardener went back inside and shut the door, her mood altered by the threatening weather, and so she missed all the drama.

"Get out of my way"!" shouted the sun to the harvest moon. "This is my world, not yours!"

"I'm fed up only shining at night when everyone is in bed," answered the moon, standing up for herself for once, "Why can't I have a bit of the daytime?"

"Look," bellowed the sun, "it's not my fault if people prefer me to you! I don't send them crazy when they look at me."

The moon thought that this was very unfair.

"And I don't frazzle them to a cinder!" she said in a sob. At this her cousin, the tide, reared up furiously, the clouds burst in chagrin and the rain began to lash down so that all the plants in the garden were blinded and bent.

In the morning garden both blackcurrant and bramble huddled down as far as they could.

"I say," whispered the blackcurrant, "it looks a lot drier down there by the next door shed. Would there be any room for me?"

"Get lost!" said the bramble (because he was a bit like that), "You wanted your place in the sun, didn't you? No wonder your leaves are all dried up now and your berries all gone. Look at me – my leaves are still green and juicy and my berries are just turning ripe."

The blackcurrant looked up uneasily at the sky. Before the bramble had moved next door it had used to shelter him a little, rather grudgingly, it is true, but efficiently all the same. He felt very exposed now. There was no point in looking at the redcurrant beside him. She had paled into insignificance long ago, and this summer her berries had, as usual, been meagre. The blackcurrant thought sorrowfully that their particular corner of the garden could be a lot happier than it was.

Why was the bramble so quarrelsome, and the redcurrant so dull? Why was the little oak tree round the corner always sad? Why, when he himself produced such wonderful berries, which the gardener made into jam, did he sometimes feel so alone?

Up in the sky the wind had risen to the defence of the sun, and was blowing the black rain clouds right away. Wind and light fought water and night, and the universe roared. The light grass in the morning garden leaned quite over, trying to keep its balance, and it was then that the big bins from the north garden fell right onto it. If even the big bins were unable to stand against this hurly-burly, what chance was there for anyone else?

"You won't beat me this time!" screeched the moon to the sun, though she had turned rather pale with the effort of displaying herself in daylight. "I'm fed up of being bullied by you!"

"Just watch me!" yelled the sun, with the wind funnelling behind him, although it wasn't long before the tide made another big rush and summoned his rain clouds right back again. The sun ducked his head, quickly, in case his ecstatic flames got put out.

To and fro they went, wind and sun and rain and sea, all morning; blow, lash, duck, gust, shine, shower, whine, wither. The moon had lost her strength now. Her new dress had been ripped to shreds by the whipping wind, and she had been drenched by the rain clouds sent by her own side. No one noticed that she had slipped away, to renew herself for when she would return in the night that was to come. The tide fell back, and the sea slashed white streaks across the waves so that they turned into a million slanted spears, glinting as they withdrew.

The quarrel raged on, without the moon and the tide, with only the clouds left now on the losing side. Showers thundered hard across the face of the wind, or, as you might say, "in the teeth of the gale". The wind bit right back, with the sun egging it on, until the angry clouds draped themselves round the tops of the hills for protection. The hills tried their best to shrug them off, rising darkly from their wraiths of mist and glowering hard across the once-bright bay; but the power of the harvest moon was not easily forgotten, and the clouds persisted, beyond the point where anyone could see that the field was lost.

Everyone in the garden was miserable. The blackcurrant, who, as you have noticed, was a very sensitive sort of chap, wondered why he even tried to be happy at all when there was so much silly quarrelling going on. He felt sure his berries would be affected.

Then a little voice wound its way to his ears. Someone was singing, softly,

"*The Lion and the Unicorn fought for the Crown,*
The Lion chased the Unicorn all round town;
Some gave them white bread, some gave them brown,
Some gave them plum cake and drummed them out of town."

The dull redcurrant bush smiled at the blackcurrant.

"The Lion and the Unicorn," she said, and shook her top branches, "Right up there chasing each other all round the town."

The blackcurrant laughed. How clever she must be to think of such a fine song!

"I'm so glad you're here," said she, confidingly, "I feel safer with you around."

All day the weather raged, and in the end, of course, the sun and the wind won the battle. In its wake was desolation. In many places the earth was scoured clean, and many leaves in their prime had been tortured, alternately scorched and beaten by sun, wind and rain. The garden lay spent and exhausted. The gardener walked around examining the damage. Only once did a smile come to her lips, when, right up at the top of the south garden, she found that the whitebeam, though bereft of nearly all its foliage now, had graced its bare branches with clusters of bright red berries. In the devastation they shone like candles, on a birthday cake that should have been.

In the evening, as twilight stole back to cover the garden's scars with her dusky gloom, the blackcurrant remarked to his friend the redcurrant bush,

"The garden is battered and the ground is covered in leaves. The trees in the south garden look quite bare."

"Look again," said the redcurrant gleefully, "Have you not seen what the great quarrel has done?"

"I can't see round far enough," replied the blackcurrant, twisting his branches as far as they would go. "Ouch! I just can't quite . . ."

"Oh, for goodness sake," put in the bramble bush, who had much longer stems and whose next door shed looked over the south garden, "Stop all that twisting and turning. She's talking about that gloomy oak tree there, the one who never opens his mouth."

"Tell me, tell me," pleaded the blackcurrant, who by now was quite consumed with curiosity.

"Well, it must have been scared out of its misery," said the bramble, actually sounding pleased, "It's held onto all its leaves when the other trees let go. And here's a secret you can keep to yourselves all night till the gardener finds out tomorrow; it's taken twenty years, but at long last it's decided to produce some acorns. Just stretch this way a little, down by my shed here, and you might just manage to see them - all new and brown and hanging on there in brave style. Maybe the great quarrel in the sky did some good after all. Cleared the air around here."

The redcurrant smiled to herself and rocked her thin stems. She thought, with all this excitement, maybe *my* berries will be a little more plentiful next summer.

8. The Harvest Moon

In the aftermath of the great quarrel, when the moon and the sun had fought for dominance in the sky, and the sun had won, the moon returned, silvering the bay so that night was turned into day. She was content with that, for every thing in nature has its place, but just occasionally the sun needed reminding that others counted too. So everyone felt better after the Dance of the Equinox, which was the name the moon preferred to give to the quarrel, except that the garden looked a little worn and used.

When she appeared that night the moon was huge and silver, aloof from all of them, with the skirts of her ball gown held high. Although she had had to renounce the daylight, she was still superbly beautiful. That was when the swirling waves called out to her,

"Don't forget we are your friends! Lend us your magic, so that men may forget they have legs and are bound to the earth! Enchant them with your silver moondust, so that they lean out from the decks of their ships and wish to become one with us!"

But the moon only smiled, and continued on her way. As morning drew near she turned herself to gentle gold, and blessed the garden with peace. Then she slipped from sight, as the sun's early brilliance stroked the sky to the east.

The gardener stood on the doorstep, in the morning garden.

"I wish you could see this," said the boisterous Escallonia, which formed a tall hedge against the sea winds, to the piece of old tree stump low in the ground beside it. The old root had belonged to a Scottish Rose, which had once graced the entrance to the garden with its small pink blooms, now seen no more.

"I don't know about graced," thought the gardener (because at the time of the harvest moon she could hear what the plants were saying to each other) "it certainly *grazed* people's arms and legs when they came in the gate. There is a difference."

51

The rose root sighed. It wasn't its fault it had been put in the wrong place, and had therefore had its branches all cut back, so far that it felt it would never recover.

"See what?" it muttered grumpily, in response to its overbearing neighbour.

"The Pirate Island," replied the Escallonia, "which sits at the curve of the earth, called the horizon. You cannot always see it, but today is a magical day. The Pirate Island has borrowed the colours of the sea

52

and sky, and is blue-grey against the pink of the sun's long arm that reaches round the headland. To the east the sun's arm is wider, for at this time of the equinox he rises exactly there; but he stretches right to the south-east, past the sheltering hill." The Pirate Island looks like a great sailing ship, set on a flying carpet in the sky!"

"How can that be?" asked the poor rose root from his corner down by the gate. The Escallonia, which, you know, was always too big for its roots, had completely   taken over his space, and even dominated the sky above him, so that he could see nothing of the magical Pirate Island. He felt that since his roses were gone life was slipping him by, and that he had no more part in it.

"It is the effect of the horizon, the curvature of the earth," the gardener was saying softly to herself, as she stood with her cup of meadowsweet tea in her hand. "The island looks just as if it is curved up at either end, just like a ship!" Had she heard the Escallonia, or did she just happen to be thinking the same thing? Who knows?

"I will describe it to you," continued the Escallonia eagerly. "Just beside it, to the east, where the sun is still shaking his forelock like a

53

great horse, are the candles of the morning, the clouds that bathe in his light and so become brilliant white, pink-hued, or even, as now, encircled with gold. They are ranged along the horizon like angels guarding the earth."

"It must indeed be beautiful," said the rose root rather drily, although if you listened hard (as the gardener might have been doing) you could hear a note of wistfulness in his voice. He would never see such things now, nor feel his long stems bask in the warmth of the sun and uncurl their delicate pink flowers.

So the garden entered a morning of calm and delight. The leaves which had cavorted the whole of the previous day in the equinoctial gale were gathered up by the gardener and trundled away in her shiny green wheelbarrow to their special place right at the back of the neglected trees in the evening garden. There they rested and sank down into the soft earth, to be altered and transformed. In the spring they would return to their trees, feeding the new growth with their rich mulch. The little oak tree was already showing new little buds. They were not acorns, as the redcurrant bush and the bramble had thought, the day before; even the magic of the harvest moon could not produce such a miracle. The little oak needed the sun after all; and he also needed a companion in the world. The gardener thought of this as she passed him again and again, with her barrow full of the harvest of leaves.

At last all was tidy in the garden and the sun frolicked along in great joy to play among the trees, whose branches he could now finger, and kindle with his golden light. Even the bramble poked his head out from the wall of the next door shed, and produced a gorgeous black berry, large and rich and full (but still not very tasty, thought the gardener). She left him alone. It was not his fault he had been in the wrong place in the garden, and now had to live out his life in the narrow gully between the fence and the next door shed. The bramble was large and pushy and could cope. The rose root, on the other hand . . . perhaps she had been a bit over-enthusiastic with his spreading stems. The gardener thought about the rose root and was a little sorry.

She was leaving that day on one of her mysterious sorties to the world beyond. But, because at the time of the harvest moon she knew what the garden was thinking, she went first to the little oak tree that was always sad, and promised that she would bring him back a mate to cheer him up and perhaps help him produce acorns.

Perhaps a little moondust had landed on the gardener – who knows?

The garden knew it would be a long time before she came back, because when she left she had one of those things she called a suitcase. But it was a nice rest for everyone while she was away. The gardener was always interfering, whereas if she would just leave well alone . . . but since it was the bramble who was saying this, no one listened. He really had a bit of a chip on his shoulder about his narrow bed between the fence and the next door shed.

"Hey," whispered the Escallonia, to the rose root, "Now's your chance, while she's not here to notice! Can't you grow a bit?"

"No," said the rose root, glumly, "I can't do anything now. It's too late. I'm too old, and in the wrong place. No one wants me."

The tender-hearted redcurrant choked back a sob. The normally cheery blackcurrant looked perturbed.

The Escallonia was embarrassed. After all, he was strong and hearty, and, like the sun, in the ascendant. He was not the right person to talk to the old rose root, when he himself was so busy and happy. If only there as someone who knew how the rose root felt, who had also suffered catastrophe!

The Escallonia cast his glossy eye over the morning garden. He tut-tutted in irritation as he noticed that just underneath his left foot, where the wall of the next-door house joined the morning garden, a great long shoot of the cheeky bramble had actually taken root! Even this late in the season, it had young, fresh leaves.

But what about the bramble, father of this young upstart! He had been cut down and pushed out, just like the Scottish Rose. He would know how they could help! After all, look at the comeback he'd made!

"If that gardener would just leave well alone," began the bramble, when the Escallonia's nearest leaves whispered their request to him, but the Escallonia shook itself so crossly and its top stems waved so threateningly that the bramble decided to stop complaining and listen.

"That young shoot of mine there can just scramble over and take a look," he agreed. "It's strong and healthy, and can burrow itself quite well down by that old rose root. Here, you!" he bellowed suddenly at the bright young thing that was poking its way merrily right through the nice new patch the gardener had dug to encourage the shy redcurrant, "Get yourself along there and see what state that bit of old root is in. Report back here, pronto!"

When the bramble shoot prodded at it, the rose root woke up from the nice nap it had been having. It didn't seem very interested in the bramble shoot and went back to sleep again.

"So!" said the bramble bush when the young cadet got back, "It has lots of little shoots sticking out of it, does it? That's funny. Why isn't it growing, then?"

"Well, said the young shoot excitedly, for it felt very important, "*it* isn't growing. But lots of other leaves are!! They're all bright green and raggedy-edged."

"Dandelions," said the bramble grimly, "feeding off the root. Am I right or am I right?"

"What does that mean?" asked the Escallonia, the redcurrant and the blackcurrant all together.

"It means," answered the bramble, who, although he had been wrong about the oak tree's acorns, had learned a lot in his travels, "that the old rose root will not make a comeback. No, it's terminal, I'm afraid. Nothing we can do. The day of the Scottish Rose is done. Just ask the Sweet William, who will tell you a tale of battles lost and won."

The rose root was not listening. It was feeling very tired these days, as if it had no strength left with which to be interested in the garden.

During the days that followed it seemed to the Escallonia that the harvest moon shone gently on the wrinkles of the old rose root, and that during the day the sun warmed it particularly. The Escallonia used his leaves to whisper to it little messages about the warmth of the soft earth in which the root was now mostly buried, and the bright colour of the dandelion leaves that were receiving their new life from it.

One night the root borrowed a little of the moon's light, so that it shone with a pale gleam, and said, rather feebly,

"I would have liked some children of my own; some bright bushes to bear my name."

"Oh, but you should just see," cried the Escallonia bush at once, "that down there by the shore, where the gardener empties her shiny green wheelbarrow, your cut-off branches have taken root and are flourishing!"

The redcurrant and the blackcurrant looked at it each other but said nothing. They knew that this was not true. The rose root only smiled, and the moon stretched out her silver rays along its gnarled skin.

"It's not given to us to choose what we leave behind us," remarked the bramble, judiciously. "If I were you," he shouted to the rose root, who was by now very deaf, "I'd be content with producing two million dandelions. Remember the promise that the sun made to that little dandelion who lived in the lily tub. You're making it come true."

No one was sure whether the rose root ever heard. Later, when the Escallonia talked with the others, there was general agreement that it was the rose root on whom the moon had chosen to sprinkle her silver moon dust so that the rose had fallen asleep, for ever, in her arms.

When the gardener returned she carried the new oak sapling in the gate and looked at the place where the rose root had died. No, she would have to find a different place for the new tree, where it could grow as it might.

Next day she carried away the old rose root in her shiny green wheelbarrow to the special place right at the back of the neglected trees in the evening garden. There the root could sink down in peace into the soft earth, to be altered and transformed. In the spring it would return to the garden, feeding the new growth with its rich mulch.

57

9. Little Jack Sparrow

On the sparkling sea the ferry was taking away the gardener children for a holiday.

The gardener missed them already and came outside to her washing line looking for company. So the merry sparrows, whom she fed with delicious seeds and nuts, came to chat to her from the middle branches of the yellow willow. Little Jack Sparrow even hopped onto the washing basket stone.

For the gardener children, and also for Little Jack Sparrow, the washing basket stone was not a washing basket stone at all, but a pirate stone. The gardener children would jump up onto it, hang their pirate flag from the washing pole and shout to the gardener, who was giving the grass its final cut for the year,

"Swab the decks, cabin boy! Swab the decks!"

And the gardener would ask them whether she was allowed ever to stop for a cup of coffee, and they would shout,

"No, no stopping! No cups! Swab the decks, cabin boy!"

And when they had gone Little Jack Sparrow would jump up there too and chirp,

"Swab the decks, cabin boy! Swab the decks!"

Mother Sparrow, on the other hand, did nothing but hop around the garden pleading with her son Jack to be careful. That is, when she wasn't flying around looking for him, finally finding him hiding from her, amongst the twisted old tree roots, or perched right at the top of the sunny yellow willow, who always enjoyed a good game. Then there would be nothing for dinner and little Jack would complain at the top of his voice until the other mother sparrows all thought that Jack's mother was just not up to scratch.

Scratch she did, though. She worked ceaselessly whenever Jack was behaving himself, which wasn't very often. She searched assiduously for insects and grubs for him – he was especially partial to a nice fat cleg, or horsefly. Of course, since the horse had said goodbye, there weren't too many of those to be found. There were, however, lots of scurrying black beetles about, since the gardener had cut the grass. Mother Sparrow had just found one and was carrying it to Jack in her beak, where she had left him safe under the hawthorn, when, of course, she saw that, as usual, he wasn't where he was supposed to be.

"Jack Sparrow!" she called out in her crossest chirpy voice, catching the beetle with her left foot as it tried to beetle off into the long grass. "Jack Sparrow! Come here at once!"

No answer. Mother Sparrow scurried then, just like the beetle, who made good his escape. What a naughty bird Jack was! She ran up and down the nameless yellow flowers at the top of the south garden, which was a favourite place of his, because from there you could look out on the sparkling sea and the Pirate Island. But no, no Pirate Jack.

She did find Father Bird, who was busy with a red berry he had carried all the way from the whitebeam tree. The whitebeam tree, whose true name was Flashing Messenger, nodded with pleasure when the sparrows came to enjoy the feast he provided for them. He was generous-hearted, if somewhat given to gossip. On this occasion he leaned his laden branches downwards as far as he could in order to hear the marital quarrel that looked likely to ensue.

"Father Sparrow! Just what are you doing sitting there pecking at a berry, when our son is at large in the world and in grievous peril?"

Father Sparrow, who had not attained his advanced age without learning how to be careful, had not missed his wife's arrival. All the time he had been enjoying the bright red berry he had been cocking his head from side to side to listen, and bringing his head up sharply every second or two to keep an eye on whoever, or whatever, might be approaching. Danger lurked everywhere in the garden, for a small brown bird, even one with such a fine black bib as Father Sparrow had.

Mother Sparrow knew what a careful look-out he kept and so it annoyed her intensely when Father Sparrow ignored her outburst and calmly went on pecking at his berry.

"Men!" she screeched at him, "I don't know why we bother with them. It's all very well for you, fathering chicks – you don't worry too much about bringing them up, that's clear!"

"He's not a chick any longer," replied Father Sparrow somewhat indistinctly, his beak full of juicy berry, "he's a fledgling, which means he has to go out in the big bad world. He has to learn to make his own mistakes."

"Oh, how can you be so heartless?" cried poor Mother Sparrow, "If he makes a mistake it'll be the end of him! Oh, Jack, Jack, where can you be?"

61

"We can see him," chirped the other mother sparrows, who were still chatting in the middle branches of the yellow willow. "The whitebeam's just passed on the message that you're looking for him. Can't say we were surprised, of course, that he's misbehaving again," and they sniffed. They preened their chests, and their own perfectly behaved fledglings, who were sitting decorously in the whitebeam tree, followed suit. They were playing at Barber's Shop, making the feathers on their heads stand up in Mohican style.

"Don't eat *too* many berries, darlings," called their mothers to them, "Or they'll give you sore tummies."

"You can see my boy Jack?" called Mother Sparrow and flew straight to the other mother birds. Father Sparrow thought about saying to her that Little Jack Sparrow had to learn the hard way to take care of himself, but closed his beak again, for he knew she wouldn't listen. And there was such a feast to be had in the whitebeam tree. Father Sparrow planned a very happy day just idling in the sun surrounded by berries. If that boy Jack had any sense he'd do the very same thing.

By this time Mother Sparrow had flown to a good high perch in the yellow willow, which was really quite bare at this time of year. She held herself high against the sky, which was cloudless and bright blue. Her pale chest puffed out with anxiety, and her beady black eye darted around the south garden.

Then she saw him, and almost fell off the branch. He had found the choicest feast in the garden. On certain days lately, with winter just around the corner, the gardener had started filling her long plastic bird feeder with peanuts. Of course everyone loved them, especially Jack, to whom his mother had brought several. But just now, here he was; he had found them for himself, and his mother could see that Little Jack Sparrow was in his element. He was having a ball. He was the only sparrow at the bird feeder, and he was king of the castle. But his mother could also see why there were no other birds there.

At the bottom of the feeder, under the old southernwood bush, crouched the bad ginger cat.

Now, the bad ginger cat did not belong to the garden. He belonged to the next door house but one. He lived there with other cats, whom you may hear about one day, but for now he had come in to the garden on his own. He had come in to the garden because he had heard about the peanut feeder. He had come in to catch birds.

And now he was lying in wait for Little Jack Sparrow.

"Jack, Jack!" called out the poor Mother Bird, "The cat!"

At first Little Jack Sparrow did not hear. He was too busy playing with the peanuts that had collected round the base of the long plastic tube. His beak was still too little to pick them up properly, so he was poking around to find the smallest one. So all the other Mother Birds added their calls, chirping at full volume from the middle branches of the yellow willow. The whitebeam flashed his leaves as best he could in the sunlight, sending out his warning semaphore, "Cat! Cat!"

Then Little Jack Sparrow looked up and saw his mother, beside herself and almost in a swoon on her top branch.

"Look, mother!" he called in joy, "I have found where the peanuts live! Isn't this fun?"

The bad ginger cat had also taken note of the cacophony from the yellow willow. It looked a little puzzled, at such a collective response, and stared malevolently at Little Jack Sparrow as he hopped about the feeder in his best carefree manner. The bad ginger cat moved slightly, ever so slightly, so that its long bad ginger tail was uncurled and it was ready to pounce when its chance came.

Now everyone was chirping at Jack, and although there were too many voices now for him to understand anything they said, it dawned on him slowly that all the mother birds were in the yellow willow, and that all his fellow fledglings were in the whitebeam tree, and also that all the mothers were chirping at him in a very cross fashion, though he could not in the least think why; and Little Jack Sparrow thought at last that there might be something he had missed.

He swung himself upside down from the feeder, and found himself staring right into the great yellow eyes of the bad ginger cat, who was looking up at him, his tail swirling and his whiskers trembling with anticipation.

All Jack knew then was that he had let go of the bird feeder platform and was falling. Indeed he knew nothing more until he hit the soft grass underneath. After that everything became a confused impression of whirling browns and orange, a strange sense of not being king of anything any more and not being able at all to do what he wanted to do, which was to fly up into the air again and find Mother Sparrow high in the yellow willow.

His tail hurt, then one of his wings. There was no time to try and understand why. His other wing was good and strong, and his beak was sharp. He could hear all the birds and all the trees in the world screaming now, and he knew he had one chance only to be King Jack, to be Jack, to be able to fly up once more into the beloved trees and perch on their dear, grainy branches. He thrust himself forward with all his strength, and broke free of the grasp of the bad ginger cat. With his bright black eye he saw that he had been under the paw of the giant beast. Now its face came nearer and its paw was raised again. Jack flapped his wing but it was not enough; he needed two, and his other wing felt quite weak and ill used. Was there nothing he could do? Was this the end of life, and summer, and joy?

The giant paw slammed down on his tail, and held him hard. The wide mouth opened, showing sharp white teeth, and a red, red tongue. Oh, where was Mother Sparrow?

Then there rose in the air a strange sound, greater than the whole orchestra of birds and huger even than the whitebeam tree's waving arms. Down from the sky (it seemed to poor dazed Jack) appeared a giant shape, waving something more terrible than any of the whitebeam's friendly twigs. It was a whole tree trunk on the move, and at its end it wore a huge bristly head! The giant shape roared out, in a voice of thunder,

"You bad ginger cat! Let that poor bird go! Get out of the garden before I take this brush to you!"

And the bad ginger cat fled, tail in the air, its fur like the bristles on the broom the gardener carried in her hand.

The mother birds stopped chirping; they had done their work. The gardener looked up into the branches of the yellow willow tree, where Little Jack Sparrow's mother darted her round black eyes nervously, unable to manage even the smallest chirp of relief. The gardener picked up Little Jack Sparrow and very gently stroked his wing. Then she laid him on the soft grass beside the pirate stone, and went to fetch him a dish of water.

She looked up into the willow tree again.

"There you are, Mother Sparrow, she said, "Your baby's all right. I don't think he'll go near the bad ginger cat again.

And next time the gardener had a visit from her friend, the man who watched the distant hills, she asked him to make the peanut feeder a little higher, and a little further away from the old southernwood bush, who had watched the whole episode with his thin, drooping leaves and who hoped never to see such a thing again in the sunlit garden.

And, as far as I know, he never did.

10. America

In the morning garden the lily in the faded pink tub, whom everyone was waiting for, had finally bloomed.

She was exotic, which means she was a rare and delicate flower that did not grow naturally in the garden. The gardener had purchased her bulbs the previous autumn, and had looked after her with great care, moving her out of the wind whenever it blew straight in from the sparkling sea. The little dandelion, who had tried to grow in the faded pink tub, perhaps in hopes of one day seeing the gentle lily, had been pushed quite out and had had to be rescued by the gardener child (but you may remember that story).

The lily's long, tongue-like petals were a rich shade of orange, with a darker blush just at her heart. She blushed a lot, mostly when people praised her great beauty and refined posture. She loved being the special one in the sunlit garden. Of course, the sun, giant of the sky, shone just for her, and laid his carpet of gold before her on the grey slate of the patio. The lily was very happy.

But she had never heard of America.

Neither had most of the other plants in the garden, but that did not bother them. They each had their place in the sunlit garden, where some of them had been for many years. In winter, when the wind raged through the trees and left them bare, nearly everyone could watch the sparkling sea, which was a great joy, for it was forever changing, and yet forever the same.

But when the exotic orange lily heard the word "America" she swept her head in sudden disarray, and did not know what to do with herself. She bent one way, and then the next, trying to listen to what was being said nearby at the swinging gate.

There were people there, men with great round tubes that they kept pointing into the trees. At first the inhabitants of the garden had been scared, but they soon saw that the great round tubes did them no harm, and were, in fact, not really pointed at the trees themselves but at the birds that lived in them.

"Bird-watchers!" whispered the bramble bush fiercely, in case anyone else got in first.

He waited until he had everyone's attention, and elaborated.

"Bird-watchers. They come with things called cameras, to take pictures of our garden. From what I can make out, they've come specially to see . . ."

"Me," thought the lily, happily, forgetting she was not a bird, but a flower.

"An American Hermit Thrush," continued the Bramble, loftily, "which has come all the way from America."

And that was how the lily first heard of America. She did not know why, when the gardener walked with the men past her tub, she trembled. She trembled not with apprehension, but with excitement, which, of course, is something quite different. Until the day her petals re-entered the earth she never forgot how dizzy she felt on that day, so that she almost needed to lie down on the golden carpet of the patio floor and bathe in the hot sunshine. Perhaps if she were to do that, one of the men would see her lying there, gorgeously, orangely exotic against the plain grey of the slate, and take her with them to America . . .

"Tell us about the American Hermit Thrush," begged the little daisies, perking up their pretty heads at all the goings-on.

"I'm trying to listen to their conversation," replied the bramble, "which I have to say I doubt any of you lot would understand." But of course he couldn't help relaying it all for them anyway.

"The hermit thrush has been blown here on the wind, across the great ocean called the Atlantic. Beyond the ocean lies the land of America, which is huger than anything you might imagine, and what is even more strange, is at the same time empty and full of people. There are many wonderful plants there, tall and ancient, and birds, of course, like this one. Despite all the interest the hermit thrush is causing round here it seems it's a shy little thing. It's been hiding just up the road there, and now this army of great big men has probably scared it off. Smaller than our thrushes . . ." he was repeating all that he could hear of what the bird-watchers were telling the gardener. "It's got a red tail! Now, has anyone seen that?" he glared round and shook his long stems at the daisies, who tucked their heads in again in alarm.

"Well, it's certainly an exotic visitor to our island garden!" came the voice of the gardener, which of course everyone understood without the help of the bramble bush.

"Exotic?" whispered the lily to herself. "But that's *my* word! I'm exotic! And this is *my* garden – isn't it?"

And she was quite upset, and quite quiet, until long after the men went away, and the garden returned to itself. The sun, giant of the sky, left them to see to his gardens on the far away side of the earth, *in America*, thought the lily, forgetting to look up one last time into the sun's jolly face before he swept down behind the sparkling sea. This was usually the lily's favourite sight, because just when he bid her goodnight he turned the sky and sea blazing orange, just for her, because of her great beauty and delicacy.

Next morning the garden woke to a new sound. The sun was just returning, but for once no one was watching him. Everyone was listening. From somewhere right in the heart of the south garden, rose a beautiful, ethereal singing, which was quite strange to them. The daisies woke up and thought they had been dreaming of baby angels with bright gold curls. The Sweet William remembered the colours of their land that they bore and thought they heard again the clear reveille of the trumpet, which used to wake the soldiers from their weary sleep. The hardy yellow willow wept for all the children it had played with all the years, who were now grown up and gone. The old southernwood bush remembered *his* youth, when he was young and green and life was a fine thing. Even the bramble bush looked more cheerful, as if he didn't *really* mind being stuck between the fence and the next door shed.

The lily in the faded pink tub felt her heart lifted up to the skies with joy. She saw rich, fantastic colours of which she had never dreamed before; she tasted on her petals the heady, heavy scent of her lily sisters in the far away land of America; she wilted under the denser heat of her friend the sun as he opened his dazzling face to the southern lands; she arched herself under the first kiss of sweet rain after the long dusty summer. The bird's music took her to the heavens, and love overcame her, for the little thrush and his entrancing voice.

Softly, softly, the gardener stole out of the wooden house. There were no men with the things they called cameras; there was only the gardener, and her garden.

She came quietly to her stone in the south garden. The American Hermit Thrush was indeed shy, and kept himself to himself, as his name suggested. He had perched on a high branch of the ash tree. The ash had never before been so honoured. He held his silver branches very still, and hushed his leaves.

The bird sang on, with the garden before him; he might have been giving a royalty performance. "Except they don't have royalty in America," hissed the bramble.

"Oh," said the lily, weakly.

The hermit thrush paused in its song, which had conjured up for the garden rain-swept rivers, snow-capped mountains, red-baked deserts and the lush, turgid forests of the south. So the gardener, on behalf of the garden, spoke to him, in a soft voice. She read from a book she had carried out with her. She told the thrush that the words had been written about him, by a man called Walt Whitman, who was American.

"Was he one of the birdwatchers?" cheeped out a young daisy.

"Ssshh!" said everyone.

In the swamp in secluded recesses
A shy and hidden bird is warbling a song.
Solitary the thrush,
The hermit withdrawn to himself, avoiding the settlements,
Sings by himself a song.
Song of the bleeding throat,
Death's outlet song of life, (for well dear brother I know,
If thou wast not granted to sing thou would'st surely die.)

And the lily, listening, felt herself grow faint with the words, so beautiful and sad, in case they were for her too.

O wild and loose to my soul!
O wondrous singer!

"Why am I here, and not in America?" she cried out, but no one heard. "My throat too will bleed! When the harsh east wind comes from the sea, which on that day will not be the sparkling sea, what will become of me? I am too fine for this land, not like the bramble there, so pushy and strangling everyone, or like those daisies that peek out commonly from all over the place. I will not survive here! I must go to America, with the beautiful singing thrush! Take me with you, beautiful bird! Take me with you!"

"I am only a thrush and my song is for me alone," he seemed to reply, in his song. And the gardener closed her book and sat on her stone and remembered the days when, long ago in her youth, the singing people had come from America, to weave their spell over her and the others in her life's garden then; so that many of the people from her country, like uprooted flowers, left their homes and went *to look for America*, as they sang, to the land across the wide ocean where heights of skies cascaded into depths of chasms; where a handful of dust from the side of the road became a song that could carry travellers along the lonely miles, as the hot sun burned, and the trail ran white into the blue hills.

That day the hermit thrush flew away, taking his song who knew where, perhaps to become part of the orchestra of the shore, where the sparkling sea scoured smooth the faces of pebbles with its waves; or maybe to lift the hearts of tired workers in the fields far from their homes, and make them remember things gone, or long for things to come. The hermit thrush left, and no one seemed to mind, except for the lily.

She could not speak of it; so she turned her petals yet a deeper shade of orange, and with her beauty challenged the sun that she would be brighter than his sky at sunset. She drenched the garden with her scent, for she was dreaming of the dense forests where dwelt her sisters, whom she would never know; for it is said that, above all things, scent is the straightest path to memory, and to secrets learned and understood, without words, and without song, for ever.

Walt Whitman, from *When lilacs last in the dooryard bloomed.*

11. The Witch's Gift

The garden woke to a morning of steel-grey November light and a slate-coloured sea, which matched perfectly the slate on the patio. The blessed geraniums shivered in their green pot. They were blessed because, no matter how cold the weather, or what season of the year it was, their pot contained the heart of colour, sometimes a mere vestige, but always a promise. Today, even the geraniums looked rather thin, and bloodless. Their stems struggled to hold them up, but they held their heads high, and peeked through the still-luxuriant Escallonia to see what the morning might bring.

Finally it brought the sun, giant of the sky. It was evident from the first that he had been partying. As the bramble put it, he had been out on the tiles. No one was quite sure what that meant, but it sounded good, and only Little Jack Sparrow uttered a kind of nervous titter when he thought that the only other creatures he knew about who did this were cats. The bad ginger cat still served as a warning to him to be careful whenever he went out to play; and so, his father remarked, in a way it had been a useful ginger cat. Jack wasn't too sure he agreed with that, so he put the cat out of his mind and hopped onto the green pot to see what the geraniums were looking at.

The first tentative rays of the sun, who was feeling a little fragile after his party on the other side of the world, stole out raggedly from behind thick grey clouds. They decorated the tops of the clouds with pink, so that wavy lines stretched across the sky like left-over streamers from party poppers. The sun, feeling the beginnings of a headache, poked about in his gorgeous palette and, with a rather shaky finger, painted in the gaps between the clouds, so that here and there the sky was patchy pink or orange, depending on whether he had his eyes properly open or not. Sometimes it was hard to tell whether the sky was pink, orange, or both.

The geraniums, with their superior knowledge of colour, were consulted on this important question. Did the small patch of sky to the east there match the dusky pink of the tallest geranium?

"No, not at all!" decided the bramble, poking his stems in as usual, "You're too slow at making up your minds. It's turned red now, like that littlest one of you with hardly any petals left."

At this censure the poor little red geranium hid himself right down in his pot, and bent his neck.

"It's not his fault!" said Jack Sparrow, who among all his faults had the virtue of standing up for other people. He owed this virtue to his father, who, in Jack's opinion, was always criticising him, with the result that Jack knew only too well what it felt like to have someone make disparaging remarks. "It's too cold for flowers!" And he fluffed his feathers out round the stem of the red geranium, who felt he had a friend, and opened himself up again.

"Look! You're missing the show!" cried the Escallonia, "The whole sky is turning red now! It's glorious!"

"It must have been quite a party," commented the bramble, drily. Jack wasn't really paying attention. He had come across a strange creature that he had never seen before, long and wriggly.

73

He wondered whether it would be good to eat, and, if not, whether it had a face and could be a friend. But now he looked up and saw that the Escallonia was right. The sky had suddenly blazed red, and the slate-grey sea turned pink, as if the sun had washed his paintbrush in it. Jack hopped in excitement, and the strange creature, oblivious to the doings of the sun, buried itself deep into the earth.

"The sea is pink just like us!" cried the blessed geraniums.

"And the sky is red like me," said the littlest geranium, and didn't mind that no-one was listening.

The sea, which the garden called "The Sparkling Sea", did not always sparkle, as everyone well knew; but when naming it they had chosen to concentrate on its prettiest qualities. It was not sparkling this morning; it was rather glowing, with an ethereal light, a light that the garden felt could not be matched, even by the sun who had given it. Its waters were still and even. No ripple, or fleck of white foam, recalled to the garden the life and energy of its waves. No beating of the waves against the rocks on the shore reminded the garden-dwellers of the force of the spray that sometimes got past the Escallonia's guard to flick a stinging saltiness onto the plants that were rooted there, at its mercy.

The sea glowed, from the stillness of its depths, which the sun had kissed, and released a tiny sliver of magic, which only the Escallonia, from his glossy height, could glimpse.

The Escallonia rustled his splendid branches, wondering whether he should tell the garden what he knew. Only he, with his spectacular view of the garden and sea, was aware that the red sky had begun to fade, and the pinkness of the sea steal away; only he had noticed the growing whiteness of the horizon as the sun dressed himself in his winter cloak; and at the moment where the light and movement of the universe altered, so, in an instant *She* was there; The Silver Witch.

Of course the Escallonia could not actually see her. The morning was already too bright for that. Rather he felt her presence as she slipped past him, and he wondered where she was going. What she was going to do in the south garden? Although at the top of it you could look at the sea, no-one in the bottom of the south garden, near the wooden house, ever saw the unearthly beauties of the sunrise. They were too enclosed. The little oak tree, for instance, had been known to ask the Escallonia what it was like when the sun came to be born every morning; and the Escallonia had felt his good heart crack.

He had always felt sorry that other people could not be in his own prime position. It was as if he had been too specially favoured, with his wonderful view to the east. He wished that everyone in the garden could see the dawn, and that it would cheer them, in particular the little oak tree, who was always so sad.

The Silver Witch passed by and back again in the smallest stream of whirling air, and was gone. The Escallonia shook his glossy leaves, with a sigh. The last of the magical red faded from the sky and the sea; but when he looked down at the green pot it seemed to the Escallonia that the little red geranium was really the brightest flower in the pot, and the healthiest too. He and Little Jack Sparrow were having a rare time together, watching a fat old black beetle climbing up the pot towards them.

"Should I push him off?" asked Jack.

"No," answered the red geranium, whose heart now overflowed with love. He will complement my red perfectly. It is important, in a pot, to have all colours and all joy."

"*Chippa!*" said Jack, without understanding a word, and off he flew, up to the top of the south garden, where his father spent his days munching whitebeam berries. He wasn't there; but the whitebeam tree, whose true name was Flashing Messenger, sent him an urgent message in his leafy semaphore.

"Look! Look! Under the Gentleman Fuchsia! Look under him!"

Jack flew over straight away. The Gentleman Fuchsia, which was not as well cared for as the Lady Fuchsia at the bottom of the south garden, was quite scraggy and bare, and it was quite easy to see the peculiar object the whitebeam tree was trying to tell him about.

The thing was the second new creature Jack had met that day, and just as mysterious as the first, although it did not disappear underground when Jack blinked at it, just to test it. It was small, not even as big as Jack, and perfectly round. The other strange thing about it was that it appeared to have no colour; nothing to match the red geranium, anyway. It didn't look dangerous, so Jack hopped around it, his head cocked to one side just as he had seen his father do, his streetwise eye keeping a sharp look-out for the bad ginger cat.

"Morning!" chirped Jack, brightly, "How do you do?", for his mother had brought him up to be polite.

The new arrival said nothing. It didn't move, or otherwise acknowledge Jack's presence. Jack, having met with no obstacle to his curiosity, peeked underneath its bland, inscrutable surface. Hmmm! It was darker under there, brown and ridged. It had a stem, quite a thick one, too, so it must be a plant. There was something funny about it, though, apart from what appeared to be an inability to converse.

"What shall we do with it?" wondered Jack. "I must go and tell the geranium about it. Perhaps he will know what to do."

The red geranium surprised Jack by being immediately very sorry for the new arrival. "It has no colour!" he exclaimed, in horror and pity, "And no home, such as our own dear green pot!" And his full heart bled for the stranger.

"No home?" wondered the Escallonia, who was listening with all his leaves. "A new arrival, with no home? And he sent Jack straight back to the top of the south garden, to find out as much as he could.

"What's your name?"

'Where did you come from?

'What do you do?

'Where's your mother?"

Jack chirped and chirped, but not a word did the visitor answer. At last Jack gave up and hopped a little way off, to pick up a whitebeam berry. Once again he had the feeling that there was something strange about the new plant, something he had missed. Jack remembered only too well the feeling of having missed something. It was the same feeling that he had had when it had suddenly dawned on him that danger lurked at the bottom of the bird feeder, in the shape, as it had turned out, of the bad ginger cat. Now he had the same feeling again, but without the same sharp sense of danger. He had a quick look around to make sure that danger wasn't the something he was missing, and caught the urgent flash of the whitebeam's leaves:

"Roots! No roots! It has no roots!"

Now Jack was a bird of great intelligence, and, if he seemed at times to be lacking in this attribute, it was only because he was young, and his intelligence was unformed and even sometimes unwise. In this case he knew perfectly well what "No roots!" meant. The new arrival was not a plant!

"But it has a stem!" he reported to the Escallonia, "It has a stem but no roots! What shall we do, what shall we do?" And he hopped about enthusiastically, enjoying the whole adventure immensely.

The Escallonia frowned, and was quiet so long that Jack had time to find out where the other funny creature had gone, down where the old rose root used to live. It popped its head – if it was a head – out briefly and burrowed down again with impressive rapidity.

"Nothing," replied the Escallonia, at last. "We do nothing. This is a gift from The Silver Witch herself."

The garden let out a collective gasp of wonder.

"None of you saw her," said the Escallonia sternly, "but she came all right, at the exquisite moment when the colours of the sunrise fuse into the white of the winter day. She has left this gift for the south garden, which is not as favoured as we are, and we will wait, and see what it does."

It was later in the morning, when the sun had managed to scrape out the last bits of autumn yellow from his palette and throw them onto the garden, that the gardener came out, with the eldest gardener child, who was tall and slim, just like a flower herself, with long, straight petals of shining copper. The gardener noticed with pleasure that, at last, the leaves of the little oak, which he was always frightened to relinquish, were edged with a light ochre; and that the Lady Rosa Rugosa had turned a dull gold, and was having a bit of a rest at last from clambering over everything with her shoots. It was while they were at the old south garden fence, inspecting the Rosa Rugosa's incursions into the garden during the summer, that the gardener child noticed the new arrival.

"A new plant!" she cried.

"No, said the gardener, "It's not a plant. It has no roots. It's a fungus. It's a mushroom! I have never had a mushroom grow in my garden before. I wonder why it has come now?"

77

"It's not really a mushroom," said the gardener child, who knew many clever things, sometimes more than the gardener herself. "It's a webcam".

"What's a webcam?" asked the gardener, feeling a little dated.

"A webcam," announced the gardener child importantly, "is a camera that can see across the whole world. It is round, just like this, and exactly the same size. It has a seeing eye that can capture anything that is happening, anywhere at all, even where we can't see, and show us it, right then!"

The gardener smiled.

"A seeing eye," she said, "like this one?" And she showed the gardener child a tiny hole in the surface of the mushroom that had been nibbled out of it, perhaps by the creature that had escaped Little Jack Sparrow.

"Just like that!" replied the child with a knowing air. "It's a camera lens. It is pointing down into the bottom of the garden. It is going to show them all the things they miss because our wooden house is in the way."

"Including the sun's rising, and all the colours he has in his palette," thought the Escallonia, "which they never saw before. So that was The Silver Witch's gift!"

"She was probably at the party too," said the bramble, whose long stems had twined themselves right into the heart of the Escallonia, because, to give him his due, he was trying to learn from someone wiser than himself.

The Escallonia smiled and nodded his great head.

"The little oak tree will be happy now," he replied, "And will someone tell that young fellow Jack that sparrows do *not* eat worms?"

12. The Herald

In the south garden, where the children played house under the abundant Oleria bush, a baby green shoot stirred herself from sleep and poked her head out from her bed of brown earth. Every day she poked her head out a little more, for she was growing strong in the rich earth and had become so clever that she now knew what daylight was, and had, for many days now, felt her tiny leaves warmed by the stupendous arrival each morning of the sun, giant of the sky.

But this morning everything in the garden was different, and the little shoot felt different too; quite warm, and even a little protected, but somehow also laid open to everything around her, in the glistening resonance of white that had covered the garden while she had been asleep. She felt as if her very soul lay bare to the heavens, and all the garden held out its branches to the hugeness of the universe.

"Oh!" she squeaked, in fear and delight, "What is it, oh, what is it?"

The Oleria, who was really very large, and still something of a stranger to the baby shoot, laughed so that his leaves quivered; and as they shook the little shoot felt tiny drops of moisture fall onto her.

"Oh!" she cried again, in surprise.

"There now!" came the voice of the Oleria, from the depths of his thick brown trunks (he had never learned to count and didn't know how to stop growing; he had, in fact, no fewer than seven solid trunks, which were so low that the gardener children could sit on them, and play house among them). "There now!" he rumbled, "This is the first snow; and you are the herald of it!"

"I, the herald?" thought the little shoot, "I wonder what that can mean?" But the Oleria bush had no time to tell her more, for at that very moment the garden trembled to a thunderous sound. None of them had ever heard such a loud noise before, and each leafless branch of rowan and willow leaned forward breathlessly to discover what it could be. The rowan and the willow were not scared, because they knew they were loved and protected in their south garden, and useful too, because the birds hid in them when the bad ginger cat came or even when the gardener herself appeared. They were able to be brave.

It was the old southernwood bush who spotted her first – for it was indeed the gardener who was making the great booming noise that caused the trees and plants to tremble to their very roots. As she turned Snail Corner, where the southernwood bush lived, everyone could see that the noise came from the enormous crunching noise she was making with her feet as she walked in the snow. It was deliciously terrifying to the garden, because although they knew their gardener would do them no harm, this snow was obviously a great power. It had arrived as silently as the gentle rainbows of autumn; but now that it was here it thundered like a god.

"Don't be afraid," rustled the scented privet, whose leaves always stayed green like the short, stubby points of the baby shoot. "It is only Winter who has come for a visit. His cloak is formed of the drops of rain that we loved when it made the autumn rainbows against the sun. Now that the sun has turned his back on us to warm other lands, Winter has frozen the colours of the rainbow all together into the white of his cloak. He wears it now in all its brilliance."

Then the privet sighed a little, for her branches were quite heavy with the weight of Winter's cloak, and her leaves, starred with his snowflake jewels, felt crisp and yet fragile, as if they balanced on a thin stem that danced between life and death, between warming sun and deathly ice.

To the baby shoot the scented privet looked like a snow angel. She waved her delicate green leaves, strangely luminous in the white snow, and more beautiful than ever.

"I wish I were as lovely as that," thought the baby shoot. The scented privet looked so enchanting that the baby shoot decided to ask her the important question.

"Excuse me," she cried, wishing her voice wasn't *quite* so squeaky, "but what is a herald?"

The privet smiled and her long stems curtseyed charmingly to the baby shoot, who curled her leaves with pleasure.

"Why, a herald tells you what is going to happen," she replied, "A herald brings the news, and tells it to all whom he meets."

"I am The Herald of the Snow," replied the baby shoot, a little sadly. "The Splendid Oleria said so."

The scented privet shook her leaves, sending a fine spray of snow over the quiet old southernwood bush below.

"I wouldn't listen to a thing he says," she replied, daintily. "He is from a land far away, right on the other side of the earth where the sun is showing his face right now, a land known as Australia. I don't know what he's doing here at all. He calls himself a holly tree, a tree of winter, yet his leaves are quite without prickles. *He* does not know about winter, or snow."

82

"Oh," said the baby shoot, "that's good. I didn't want to bring news of the snow. That is not what I do."

"What do you do, then?" asked the old southernwood bush, who spoke little but listened to everything that was said.

"I don't know yet," replied the baby shoot, "but I am not a herald of winter or the snow."

The gardener was crunching noisily through the south garden. As she went she stopped to inspect everyone who lived in it. The patio tubs, which she had moved round from the morning garden for warmth, were heavily lidded with snow, so that they looked as if someone had placed a white plate on top of them. The gardener nodded with pleasure at the white blossom of the scented privet, and lingered for a moment by the privet's neighbour, the little oak tree. He had clung bravely to his leaves right till the end, but today he had no more than a few dozen left, raggedy brown-gold wisps that fluttered bravely as more snowflakes began to fall from a sky that was made of grey steel. The gardener caressed his trunk gently, noting how the snow had nestled in its hollows and crevices, and told the little oak tree again, as she often did, how she loved him best in the whole garden. No one was jealous of the oak tree, because he was gentle, and because he tended to sadness.

While she stood quietly beside the oak, everyone could hear the sea, which lived just beyond the garden. No one could fail to notice that the waves that threw themselves against the shore were louder today, in the world of snow. It was as the snow had blanketed out all that was familiar and ordinary, all the little lives that bustled about the garden, and only the large and powerful reigned. The gardener herself, as she stood in the falling snow, was becoming quite white, as if she also were spellbound.

The baby shoot shivered, not from cold, but from a sense of mysteriousness and reverence. It was strange that this snow, itself so cold, should be keeping her bulb and her little shoots nice and warm. And what did it mean, that she had been called the herald of it? It could not be true. She must find out for sure, for it seemed to the baby shoot that this would be a heavy responsibility, and a burden, to someone as tiny as she.

The gardener had moved now to the oak tree's neighbour on the other side, the spreading hazel. She seemed worried that the hazel's reddish bark was torn, and the baby shoot wondered if this was the work of Winter in his icy march through the garden. She was certain that she was not destined to be the herald of ice and death.

The copse had become a place of great stillness, where only a single blackbird moved, flitting from tree to tree as the gardener approached. Then a robin darted out from the shelter of the fuchsia bush, his red breast heart-stoppingly bright against the white snow.

The gardener stood still, so that he would not be scared, and would go to the bird feeder, and the baby shoot held her breath because the gardener's great boots were no more than an inch or two away, and death was suspended over her.

She squeaked her distress, but the gardener could not hear. The robin heard and flew off, where the gardener would not see him, back under the fuchsia bush. The baby shoot felt sorry that she had alarmed him, and almost hid herself down under the snow. But no, her only chance of escape from the gardener's boots was to make herself seen. She thrust upwards with all her strength, the points of her green shoots striving towards the steely light. Oh where was the sun, her friend, who made her so strong and green? Her shoots were bright green against the white, and she was so tall, so tall, rising up from the snow and the cold . . . if only the gardener would see her there!

She squeaked as loudly as she could, "I am growing! I am green! Can't you see me under the snow?" although she knew the gardener would not hear. But the robin heard, and this time flew to her, flashing his bright red breast so the gardener would look their way. As she bent down, he flew off again, but the gardener had at last seen the baby shoot.

"Ah, the herald of spring!" she cried, and her great boots crunched back from the tiny shoot. "You, little one, with your green shoots, are the first sign that the sun will come back again, and winter does not last for ever!

And she went back into her house, with spring and sunshine in her heart, the gift of the baby shoot.

"The Herald of Spring!" Not of the snow, but of the spring!" The little shoot's heart was glad, and she was greener and more joyous with every breath. "I knew I did not bring the snow!"

The gardener could not hear, but the robin heard, and flew back towards her. The robin noticed many things, and understood the importance of being a friend, even to those he did not yet know. He stopped beside the baby shoot, and looked at her sideways from his bright eye.

"You are the herald of spring. In the time of the snow, you are the first to show new green. You tell us spring will come soon, and with it the warmth of the sun. But you are also the child of the snow, and in its memory you will bear a flower, as white as the snow that is the kiss of death. You are the flower of life-in-death. You are the Snowdrop."

And the snowdrop curled her little pointed shoots, and curtseyed to the robin, just as the scented privet had shown her how to do. Then she snuggled down into the warmth of the snow, to prepare the flower that would seal into its petals all the perfection of Winter's brilliant cloak.

13. The Flower Box

The clever son had made the gardener a shed, just where she wanted it, in the north garden by the neglected trees, and she was very happy. Her shiny green wheelbarrow had a home at last and would no longer turn to rusty brown when it rained, crying tears of blood where its bright new paint had flaked and torn.

The neglected ash trees, too, were lined up now to receive their share of all the attention. The gardener looked at them carefully and wondered whether they would like to have strawberries planted between them, not too shaded by their branches but set just where they would suck the richness of the soil that lay at the root of the trees, and turn it into juicy red strawberries for the gardener children.

"Hmmm!" said the gardener, and thought about what she would do with this interesting new corner of the world. Queen Meadowsweet, as she leaned gracefully through the wooden fence from her palace outside the garden, thought that when her flowers were full she might allow some of her seeds to fall into the garden; after all, you never knew what might happen now that the shed had banished the north wind. She inclined her head, as queens do, in approval; but the gardener was not looking at her.

As an artistic stroke, the clever son had also built, on the side of the shed that was sheltered from the flailing north wind, a flower box. It was large and was painted just the same colour as the shed itself, so it looked as though the shed too had become a living part of the sunlit garden. The gardener wondered what she would do with the flower box. She had never had one before. The garden generally did much as it liked, especially when she wasn't looking, and apart from the tubs on the patio in the morning garden, everything grew where it pleased in the succulent earth and spread about just where it wanted to go. The gardener thought about the flamboyant Rosa Rugosa, which surged everywhere and *would* keep coming through its wire fence into the garden; but then that was hardly surprising, for it had been born there, and everyone wants to pay a visit to the place where they were born.

The flower box was just a box. It was not alive, as the trees and plants in the garden were. The gardener did think, however, when she emptied into it a large sack of compost, that the flower box sucked it in rather greedily, as if it just couldn't wait to bust forth with life.

The gardener couldn't wait either. She went back into her house and came out with a very old and faded packet of seeds.

"Hmmm!" thought the gardener, "it's too late to sow these and they will never grow. I don't even remember what they are." But she sowed them anyway, then fetched her big green watering can and gave them a long drink. "You never know what will happen," she said to the shy ash tree, who blushed in surprise. It had been a long time since the gardener had talked to him. The sprawling willows that the clever son had cut down in order to make room for the shed had, in the exuberance of their growth, rather obscured the shy ash tree. Since their demise his world had changed, and he could no longer hide his pale branches. In fact he could no longer control them very well. Now that they had space, and light, they seemed to have a life of their own, and waved about quite randomly. To be honest, the shy ash tree was not a little embarrassed at their newly-acquired boldness.

"It's as if they've never learned their manners," he thought despondently, but he was not quite sure how to go about teaching them. They were already quite big, and becoming more unruly every day.

He hid amongst his leaves, and wondered what life would be like with the shed to shelter him from the cruel north wind in the coming winter. He could not imagine this, because the wind had turned the edges of his leaves all black on his north side, and with them his imagination too had shrivelled.

"Well!" said the gardener again, "I don't suppose they'll grow." And she went inside to cook the clever son his dinner.

That night the north wind looked into his old haunts. When he saw the new shed he became restless and cross. People were always banishing him and he didn't know why. He stalked around for a while in the more open reaches of the meadows beyond the garden, although he did not feel robust enough at this season to go too near the palace of the queen of the meadows. Those nettles that guarded her had a bit of a sting if you got too close to *them.*

It was at this moment that The Silver Witch came across him. She was stepping in her silver gown through the new iris. She was checking to see if the thick, strong leaves had grown enough for the corncrake to live there, now that the nettles were growing old and thin. The corncrake was special to The Silver Witch, because it did not live long and the grassy places where it lived were disappearing; she wanted its short life to be a happy one. She heard the north wind grumbling. He

88

sneaked round the corner of the shed every now and again to see if he could find a nice icy path over to that flimsy ash tree he liked to tease – but what was this?

A new flower box!

"Ha!" thought the north wind. "We'll see about that! Flower box, indeed!"

He blew as hard as he could, but try as he might he couldn't get round quite far enough to blow onto the flower box and chill the seeds. The Silver Witch was standing in his way, on the east side, where the bright sun would come up in the morning. She stood tall and straight, her hair in shining arcs all around her head; and she waved her wand over the flower box, and sang to the tiny seeds a song of birth, and growth, and warmth.

On the other side stood the shy ash, towards the west, where the sun would sink low at the end of the day and just bathe the seed-bed in the last of its evening light. He was keeping guard there. Although he had never been told that his name means "spear", he must have known it deep down, because at that moment he was surprised to find that he felt just like a brave warrior.

The north wind was surprised and flummoxed, turned his face huffily away and whipped off to a place where he knew he would find friends.

The north wind's friends were the bad ginger cats.

Since the story of Little Jack Sparrow there were more of them. They had bred. They had had babies. They had brought their cousins over from China. They had taken over the marches of the night. They were so sneaky that they would wait until The Silver Witch had paid her moonlight visit, and only then would they come out. Now the north wind made their fur stand up, brrr! - and they looked around, as he knew they would, for a nice newly-dug patch of earth, or an even cosier bed of compost, so they could sink down into a soft brown bed and keep warm.

"Ha, ha!" thought the north wind, "next time they go into the garden they'll find that nice warm seed box!"

He left them to do their mischief. He chuckled to himself as he raced north, to court the gorgeous, streaming aurora borealis, the northern dancers in the sky; but they too fled at his approach, and their ethereal banners of light faded at his touch. He howled, but no one listened, and so he howled the harder, and all creation turned its back upon him.

In the sunlit garden everyone had forgotten him. The next morning the gardener looked at her flower box. She looked at it before she went into her shed and she looked at it when she came out of her shed. She looked at it when she came round to see how the shy ash tree was getting on without the sprawling willows. The old willow trunk that had been left in the ground had started sprouting, and they both looked at the new, reddish-green leaves in some alarm.

"Don't worry," said the gardener, decisively, "I won't let it grow big. You are too elegant to be overshadowed by it." The ash tree blushed again, but not as much as before, for he was getting used to being spoken to by now, and was learning how to receive a compliment.

The gardener did not have to wait too long for the flower box to become a real part of the garden. One morning it was full of tiny green seedlings, their thin little stalks each graced by a pair of tiny round leaves. The shy ash nodded his own leaves in pleasure as he watched the gardener's smile.

But what was this? At the far end of the box, near the fence, the brown earth showed no tiny growth. Instead, there were the tell-tale marks of cat! The bad ginger cats had jumped onto the flower box and turned up the fresh brown earth, disturbing all the tiny plants.

"I don't think they've slept there," said the gardener to the shy ash, "they've done things there I don't really want to talk about." And she walked away crossly, because there was nothing she could do. Who could tell a cat what to do and where to go?

The ash tree did not need to be told what the bad ginger cats had done. He had seen them do it in the night. They had done their toilet, right on top of some baby seedlings, and then had scraped the earth so that the seedlings had all died. They were really bad cats. Where they had been, no seedlings would grow.

The worst of it was that the bad ginger cats had only just got started. The next day the gardener found the same thing. The only good thing about it was that the bad ginger cats had used just the same place in which to wee and poo, so that it was only at one end of the flower box that the seeds could not grow. At the other end and in the middle they were strong and healthy. The gardener still could not remember what they were but she did not mind.   They were new life, and so needed to be protected. She had got rid of the north wind, but who could tell a cat what to do and where to go?

The shy ash tree too was perplexed. Even as he thought and worried, one of the bad ginger cats was sneaking in. It pawed its way through the gaps in the wooden fence, stopped and looked around it with a hostile air. It was checking that the gardener wasn't around. She had a big broom that the bad ginger cats did not like at all.

The cat peered disdainfully at the shy ash tree. It stalked around the flower box as if selecting its spot for that night. Its stomach hung low beneath it as it prowled on its padded paws, glaring round every other moment. Then it arched its back and leaped up onto the fence above the meadowsweet, from where it surveyed the north garden.

There was not much for it to look at. The north garden, sunlit only in the early morning, was not a land of flowers. This was why the arrival of the flower box was so important. The cat did not care. It looked around for its next piece of mischief. Then a moth flew innocently out from the feathery grasses. The bad ginger cat shot out its paw to trap it – too slow; for the moth skipped instantly away from its grasp and hurtled right into the branches of the shy ash tree.

"Are you hurt?" whispered the tree to the moth. It must have been a bit stunned, because it did not answer. It was a very beautiful moth, with reddish-purple wings and a trim of ermine white at the base of the wings, just like a king, or perhaps an emperor. On each wing was a round pattern that looked just like an eye.

The moth rested on the branch of the shy ash tree and recovered from its fright, while the tree wrapped his leaves lightly around the moth to protect it. He talked to it of the bad ginger cat which had tried to catch it for fun. He told the moth about the torn and bruised seedlings which the cat had killed. The moth made no answer. The shy ash tree sighed.

"Perhaps I don't know its language," he said aloud, and was surprised to hear on the air the fritillary rustle of the Queen Meadowsweet.

"Petit paon de nuit!" she called, which is French for, "Little peacock of the night". Queen Meadowsweet was of course very good at French, as all queens are.

The peacock moth stirred and trembled. Then followed a whisper and a flutter of French that the shy ash could not understand. The moth's wings shivered, and it was off, before the shy ash had time to blink.

"We have despatched her to beat her wings at the palace of The Silver Witch, where the sun lays his head when it leaves our garden," announced the meadowsweet in her soft voice, and nodded her head in satisfaction. She did not stop there, but continued to address the shy ash tree, having recourse, as queens do, to the royal "we".

"We thank you, Monsieur le Frêne, for giving sanctuary to our royal messenger. We are indebted to you."

The shy ash was very proud indeed, although he did wonder at his new French name. He liked the rustling sound of it, and allowed his leaves just the tiniest little *cotillon*, a French jig, to celebrate.

He knew The Silver Witch would not come till night. She never did. It was when the moon rose that she was at her most powerful, when the silver spangles of her gown shone with a dazzling light, and her black hair caught the reflections of the silver orb and sent them in spears of iridescent beauty around the garden.

The shy ash tree watched and waited patiently, but even then he almost missed her. Moonlight struck the garden; one by one his branches lit up, stretched themselves, and preened their silver trunks, but still she did not come. Then, just at the moment when the moon, supreme at its moment of zenith, threw its ladder of light over the sparkling sea, she was there, standing by the shed. The ash tree watched eagerly. She had brought something with her, which she fastened gently above the flower box, underneath the roof of the shed. Then she waved her willow wand once over the flower box, so that the seeds would grow.

She came and went so quickly that she did not even pause to speak to the Queen Meadowsweet, which, thought the shy ash tree, must surely have been a great chagrin to my lady. But what had The Silver Witch brought with her? He frowned to make sense of it, and his branches lowered with the effort and the importance of it all.

"Careful!" he whispered to them, "you must practise keeping a suitable height above the strawberries that the gardener will plant beneath you. Remember always to consider others."

"But the strawberries are not here yet!" squeaked a protruding branch, and the shy ash tree raised itself up very tall and proud, so that the naughty branch had to stand straight too and behave itself.

"There are changes in the north garden," whispered the flags of yellow iris, "We remember how dull things used to be. The arrival of the flower box has been of great importance to us."

But what had The Silver Witch done? The bad ginger cats came and went as before, unimpeded except when the gardener's great broom waved its bristly head at them and they ran off with a flash of ginger tail. After all, who could tell a cat what to do or where not to go?

The north wind, however, kept away, as full summer was diffusing its warmth and light even into the north garden. The shy ash tree, since his adventure with the peacock moth and his conversation with the Queen Meadowsweet, felt so much braver and useful that he was able to keep his branches in much better control than before. Everyone in the north garden admired his new strength of character.

The ash tree was so busy growing shapely and strong and keeping his branches in order that he had stopped paying close attention to the flower box. Then one day the morning sun fell upon a splash of colour, and he saw that amongst the glossy dark green of the leaves of the box there were gleams of pink. Flowers! The cat's corner was still rather bare, and brown; but along the rest of the flower box little pink flowers raised bright little heads.

"They flowered after all," announced the gardener. "I just hope those cats don't spoil them."

She had scarcely turned her back when the bad ginger cats, two of them, appeared. The shy ash tree was sure they had been lying in wait for her to go. They both jumped up into the flower box and their tails rose into the air in anticipation of their fun. Oh yes, they knew how to spoil seeds!

But what was this? The ash tree peered incredulously through the thick new growth of his leaves. Was it only that the cats looked not so much ginger as yellow - and black – no, that wasn't right – they shouldn't be black; and what was that buzzing noise all around?

Wasps! Wasps were all around them! And they were stinging them all over!

The bad ginger cats each let out a great yowl and leapt into the air above the flower box. The swarm of wasps buzzed angrily after them, chasing them right into their own back yard.

The north garden shook with delight. The iris waved their golden flags in honour of the occasion. The ash tree allowed even his lowest branches to dance a jig. Queen Meadowsweet leaned gracefully through the fence to greet the pink flowers and hoped that she too could play host to the wasps once her own crown of blossom was upon her head.

"What's this?" cried the gardener, "Where did those wasps come from? I never had wasps before!"

She peered up under the eaves of the new shed. There, right in the corner, was a strange, whitish ball. It was made of bark, chewed thin and soft.

"A wasp's bike!" the gardener cried, "The wasps have built their paper nest here! Now those bad ginger cats will think twice before they come back!"

The ash tree nodded his branches to her, but to himself he whispered,

"The wasps didn't come by themselves! The Silver Witch brought them!"

But the gardener was looking at him speculatively, and he stopped thinking about the wasps and the bad ginger cats. After all, the gardener was the real head of operations.

"Do you know, ash tree," she said to him, "those lower branches of yours are quite a trouble to you. I think that instead of planting strawberries beneath them I will cut them off for you and we'll give you a nice little cherry tree for a companion. We could do with some more blossom in this garden – for the wasps, you know. They'll keep the caterpillars under control for me. How would you like that?"

And the ash tree shivered with anticipation, for in the north garden you just never knew what was going to happen next.

14. A New Neighbour

All round the sunlit garden the trees waved and danced as their leaves turned gold, yellow and brown in the autumn wind.

Unlike the north wind, the autumn wind was their friend. He was a happy sort of fellow, rustling and leaping about all over the place, but he knew his manners. As was appropriate, he blew a big puff of breath onto Grandfather Willow, so that his leaves were the first to decorate the lawn in front of the gardener's big bay windows. Grandfather Willow grumped a little as his branches felt the first chilly draughts, but he was really quite tough and knew that if he wanted fresh yellow leaves next spring he would have to let go of the old ones. Grandfather Willow's new young leaves were not green like those of most trees, but a beautiful soft yellow that brought out the blue of the spring sky. Across the south garden, the leaves of his cousin the red willow had bright red stalks that shone bravely now that he too was beginning to let go of his leaves; but it was Grandfather Willow that the gardener talked to when she sat her washing basket on the pirate stone, and gazed up into a cloudless blue sky framed by his golden leaves.

"She hasn't done much talking to any of us of late," grumbled the bramble bush from his corner by the next door shed. "She just picks my best blackberries and doesn't even say 'Thank you'."

"That's true," remarked the boisterous Escallonia, from round the corner in the morning garden. "I've been trying all summer to catch her attention. I've been growing as high as I possibly could, waving at her every morning when she goes to what she calls her job, and a fat lot of good *that* did. She got the man who watches the distant hills to cut my branches back. Humph!"

"There you have the problem," replied the sad oak tree. "It's that thing she calls a job. The job takes her away from us." And he curled his twin trunks together in order to hide his tears.

"There, there," soothed the sprawling Rosa Rugosa, who was lazily turning yellow and hadn't really bothered showing off her red rose hips that year, since the gardener wasn't looking anyway. "At least *you* can look through the big bay windows. I am quite exiled, so that I have to populate the waste land outside the fence! I am hoping that she will notice the defences I have put up against our enemies!", and she shuddered, because in the sunlit garden no one liked to mention the annual march of the dreaded hemlock; and next summer, if their gardener was too busy, would they be lost entirely?

"Sshh!" cried The Lady Fuchsia, "She's coming!"

But the gardener was coming only to feed the birds. She filled their seed containers and their nut basket. She checked their water and left quickly to go to the job, without even a glance at her garden children.

"She planted us!" cried the unremarkable osier willows who lived in the shelter of Grandfather Willow and who clung on to their thin leaves a bit longer because of his generosity, "And she didn't even say good morning!"

"She planted all of us," remarked an unknown tree, who normally stood very quietly beside the south fence, "and now she does not even know our names."

The sad oak tree cried softly.

No one heard him, because the cheeky privet, who was a different kettle of fish entirely from his cousin the scented privet, had started quarrelling with the second-rate osiers, who lived in the shadow of their neighbour the red willow. The privet was laughing because he stayed bright green all winter and thought he was stronger than anyone else in the garden. He had masses of white flowers like candles and had never been cut back in his whole life, even though he badly needed it. He was so cheeky that he had grown into a whole tree instead of a hedge.

"Stop pushing!" cried the osiers angrily and waved their entire branches as the autumn wind blew. They had very soft branches, which could wave like banners in the sun or droop like the flags of a lost land.

"Ha, ha!" laughed the privet, "Who's going to stop me?" And the red willow, standing between them trying to keep the peace, had to admit there was no one.

It was the same story all over the garden. The bramble, who usually didn't mind his narrow little place by the next door shed, poked his longest stem through the fence until it climbed right through the old southernwood bush. "Who is there to stop me?" said he, cockily. The southernwood didn't complain, because it had got so woody it had quite lost all its strength, and because he was right.

The purple chives, too, for the first time in their lives, felt weak and uncertain.

"She has not chopped us," they whispered, "even though she will need us to grow strong as soon as winter begins to pass."

"When will she harvest us?" asked the beetroot, and the leeks; and the baby plants from the strawberry runners wondered whether it was worthwhile even bothering to grow. They had so many dandelions, as well as the horrid hogweed, growing about them, and it was so tiring, to struggle against that all the time when one was so young in the world.

The shy ash tree in the north garden wished that the strawberries could come to him, and his trunks would help to keep the wild weeds away from the babies. But the gardener had changed her mind and said he would have a cherry tree. The season had changed and no cherry tree appeared. Had she forgotten? A cherry tree would be such a good companion!

Even The Silver Witch had not come for a very long time, which made the shy ash tree wonder. He was not so shy these days, after his adventures of the summer, and because he was not so shy he was able to think. He thought that perhaps The Silver Witch could not come when the garden was poor and neglected and quarrelsome. Perhaps The Silver Witch herself needed the strength of the garden, to weave her magic.

There was only one thing to do. The garden had to take action. And who was there to do it? No one but the shy ash tree.

The gardener visited the ash tree's part of the garden more than anywhere else these days, in order to fetch wood from the new shed. The ash made sure he stood up straight and tall whenever she came. He still had a few leaves, and he rustled them noisily, which he thought was fun, even if she didn't listen. In order to catch her eye, he turned his silvery branches so that they caught the glint of the sun. Once she looked, and stopped in her tracks, as if remembering something, but she didn't speak to him or put out her hand as she used to, to feel his smooth clean trunks and stroke them.

In desperation the ash tree stretched his beautiful branches as far as the dull Berberis who stood between him and the shed. She never said a word to anybody, and was singularly unspectacular; but she was their only hope.

The dull Berberis shrunk into herself at the mere idea of attracting the gardener's attention. What if the gardener thought of pruning her long stems? Would it hurt?

"Don't be scared," encouraged the ash tree, "We need you to do your best to attract her. And if she does cut your stems back, you will have even more flowers next year."

"Flowers?" thought the Berberis, who had quite forgotten that she could produce such a miracle. And surely, now that she came to think about it, wasn't this the time it had happened last year? The autumn wind was tickling her twigs with a zest that she suddenly found rather exhilarating. And, after all, if it helped the garden . . . She gathered all her resources together, and pushed and sprouted until, one day, to her surprise, she found herself quite covered in a charming little pink flower.

The gardener stopped on her way to the shed.

"My goodness! This poor neglected Berberis is looking lovely! I really must tidy it up. It could be quite shapely with a bit of care."

She turned away from them as if to leave again, and the ash tree's heart sank, for he could do nothing more to save the garden. But the gardener did not go. Instead she plodded carefully round the entire garden, looking at everything and everyone. She stopped at almost every tree, touched its newly bare trunk, and spoke to it as to an old friend. The ash tree's heart went out to her when she stopped at the unknown tree, for it was true that she no longer remembered its name. The garden could feel her embarrassment, for she had planted this tree, and now she remembered what the world was like when the garden had no trees, and there were no wet autumn leaves to stick to her feet and travel with her right into her house. The sunlit garden had not been a garden at all until the trees grew.

So to cover this awkwardness she apologised to the Rosa Rugosa for exiling her, and she thanked her for her work in seeing to next year's defences against the hemlock army; "for you know, with the job, I need you more than ever," she said, and the Rosa Rugosa shone gold and green with happiness in the autumn sun.

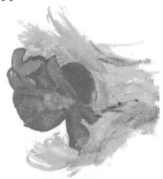

The gardener frowned at the cheeky privet and thought to herself that she would need to trim and discipline him. She patted the scented privet for her good behaviour. She admired the elegant twist of the sad oak tree's twin trunks, and for a moment he was not sad at all. The centres of his leaves were gold, framed in a wonderfully subtle green;

next to him was the spreading hazel, all aglow with her leaves just turning.

When the gardener came to Grandfather Willow she picked some of his last leaves so that she could admire their yellow stems.

"These, and the stems of the red willow across the way, will make a lovely autumn spray," she thought, and while she was about it bent down to add the long branch of bramble, with its wonderfully copper-coloured leaves, that had worked its way through the fence. It pricked her, and she said out loud, "Well, I deserve that!"

She stepped past her vegetable patch, shaking her head sadly at her neglect of it, and promised to return with her little fork. Then, with the bramble spray in her hand, and the strawberry plants patiently enduring their coat of weeds, she remembered something, which made her run right past the boisterous Escallonia, even though he had been quick to copy the dull Berberis, and had a display of jolly pink flowers just beginning.

The ash tree was slightly taken aback when she stopped in front of him.

"Strawberries or a cherry tree!" she said to him somewhat breathlessly. "Which was it to be?"

"A cherry!" whispered the ash tree, rustling his dozen remaining leaves, "a cherry tree!"

The gardener put her hand up to his trunk, and turned away wondering, because she had forgotten how to understand the language of her trees.

"You shall have both!" she said aloud. As she passed the shed, it seemed the ash tree that the autumn wind blew more strongly, so that the old, paper-thin wasps' bike gave the merest flutter, just enough for the gardener to notice it.

"It was a cherry tree," said the gardener, "for the blossom, for bees to come, and make honey."

She opened the gate to the world beyond the garden, then turned and looked round at all her garden family. She addressed the Escallonia, who lived right beside the gate.

"I can see your new flowers," she said, "and those of the fine Berberis. How lucky I am that my beautiful garden has not deserted me! I am going to visit the lady of the lamplit wood, who has a cherry tree that she will give me."

The lady of the lamplit wood! No one had ever heard of her! Did the gardener mean their Silver Witch? No, because she had no trees and no garden of her own. The Silver Witch came and went with the tides and the moon.

"Mark my words," declared the Escallonia, who, thanks to his position by the gate, knew a great deal about the outside world, "this lady of the lamplit wood will be a new influence in our garden. We must make sure we make the new cherry tree welcome."

And so they did. The cherry tree, when she arrived, was small and insignificant. She had had her branches cut severely back, and was feeling very sorry for herself, and very strange in her new home. But the shy ash tree talked to her softly in the breeze, and the dull Berberis ventured a little conversation about the advantages of the cherry tree's new situation. Messages of welcome came from the whole garden, via the whitebeam, and the cherry tree began to feel wanted, and even loved, as everyone needs to be. She leaned her thin, leafless body over the new strawberry bed and looked forward to protecting it from rough winds when her leaves grew again.

When the autumn wind went to play elsewhere and The Silver Witch came, in the spell of the harvest moon, she bathed the cherry tree's wounds in linseed oil, and told her that she would have to work extremely hard the next spring to bear pink blossom as lovely as the flowers of the Berberis. As she slipped away, round by the south garden, she put out her hand and pulled up a tangle of creeping convulvus, which during the summer she had placed around the feet of the cheeky privet, to wrap round it and stop it pushing its neighbours.

"So we had a friend after all," thought the second-rate osiers, "although we didn't know it."

Next morning the gardener came out and walked around the garden again, this time with a thin roll of paper in her hand. She stopped at the unknown tree and unrolled the drawing.

"This is a map I made when I planted you," she said, "and you, long-suffering tree, are the patient alder. I will not forget you again."

And the gardener bowed to the tree, and the whole garden smiled and rustled; for everyone needs to be appreciated, and loved, and who knew what excitement lay ahead, now that new friends might arrive from the mysterious lamplit wood?

15. Grandfather Willow

One day the sunlit garden woke to a very gloomy sky.

"It looks like rain," said Mr Blackbird to his wife, gloomily.

"Well, it is December, dear," replied Mrs Blackbird, in what we might call a conciliatory tone, which meant that she did not want Mr Blackbird to become any gloomier or blacker.   But Mr Blackbird merely cocked his eye and remarked,

"I suppose we can at least be glad it's not snowing."

"It might yet," thought Mrs Blackbird, but thought it better not to say it aloud.

Sure enough, as the morning went on, the sky became darker, and even the bramble shivered in his narrow passage between the fence and the next door shed.   When the rain came, it was thick and unrelenting.   Mr Blackbird took shelter immediately under the thin winter foliage of The Lady Fuchsia, where he had made found a nice little huddle of sticks and leaves that had stayed fairly dry.   Mrs Blackbird remained just where she was, in her favourite place below Grandfather Willow, amongst the Sweet William that even in winter would bear two or three blooms of a delicate cream and a rich, deep red.   She was conversing, in her way, and Grandfather Willow enjoyed her company as she pecked around looking for anything edible she might find that had snuggled down in his long roots, under the leaves of the Sweet William.   The Sweet William was still, even in winter, thick, and glossy green, and its promise of colour lightened even the spirits of Mr Blackbird.

"After all," he chirped to the world in general, "a garden is a garden."   Mr Blackbird, as you may have noticed, was in the habit of pronouncing, and there were times when even the loyal Mrs Blackbird was not quite sure what he meant.

"You are right!" There came upon the rain and the rising wind the cracked old voice of Grandfather Willow as his branches shook and the very last of his yellowed leaves fled. "You are right, my dear fellow! We are a garden! Each of us who lives here is part of it. It is we who make the garden, and sustain the good earth. Come here, dear bird, and sit on my branches. You would entertain me with your conversation."

But the blackbird turned his head sharply away, as a movement caught his eye just where he imagined that a beetle should be scurrying in the soft earth of the fuchsia roots.

"No, no!" he cried, "I am far too busy, and the world is cold where you are! The wind would ruffle my feathers!"

Mrs Blackbird blushed with embarrassment, to the very roots of her brown feathers.

"Men!" she twittered apologetically to the red-and-cream blossom before her.

"Don't mind," whispered the Sweet William back to her, "but do go and sit with Grandfather Willow for a bit. He feels the cold now in his old limbs."

Mrs Blackbird cocked her head to one side and looked up at Grandfather Willow. He, of course, was the real king of the garden. He was tall, although the red willow over by Snail Corner was actually taller, now that she came to notice. Grandfather Willow had the finest leaves in all the sunlit garden, but it seemed now to Mrs Blackbird that his fine limbs were looking gnarled, and his bark was a very pale colour. On sunny days in spring, the gardener loved to stand under his boughs and look up into the bright blue sky to see the new yellow of his young leaves against it, and the strong young buds just bursting through. Mrs Blackbird enjoyed this too, although of course she could look down on the yellow leaves from above and was herself part of the bright blue sky. It occurred to her for the first time to wonder whether the Gardener herself might envy her her wide blue world. Mrs Blackbird, being a creature of impulse, and always a believer in speaking her mind, found herself asking Grandfather Willow outright a question that she would never have thought she would ask.

"O Willow, Tit-Willow, Tit-Willow!" she sang, in her best winter voice. The words were those she had once heard the gardener sing from behind the French windows through which Grandfather Willow could look if he bent down.

"May I ask . . . are you quite well in this wintry spell that is upon us?

She thought she heard him cough, but it was true that it might have been . . . yes, it might just have been . . . a creak of laughter.

She looked down hurriedly in case she had been too forward. But kindness filled the air around.

"How good of you to enquire," replied Grandfather Willow, his old knees shaking as the wind blew harder and the rain turned to icy sleet, "but I have weathered many a storm, and shall weather a few more, no doubt!" And he did laugh to himself, in happiness that Mrs Blackbird had cared to ask. She hopped away, awkwardly, for it is well known that one does not turn one's back when taking leave of one's monarch, and should therefore hop backwards.

The sky grew dense and angry. Mrs Blackbird scurried to join her husband, who was pecking somewhat listlessly at a bit of twig that he considered should have been an earwig or at the very least a beetle. She squatted down in the pile of leaves that were still warm from his body, and waited for the rain to stop.

It didn't stop. It went on and on all day. Then it was night, and still the wind blew and the rain lashed down. The leaves of The Lady Fuchsia dripped around them, but she gathered her boughs tightly above them, and Mr and Mrs Blackbird stayed snugly in their leafy den while the wind blew harder and harder, whirling round and round the gardener's wooden house until Mrs Blackbird thought the gardener might get her wish and fly up high, house and all.

"At least the bad ginger cat won't be out tonight," announced Mr Blackbird, at last, grumpily. "This weather's too bad even for him."

For once Mrs Blackbird did not answer. Above the rush and tremor of the wind, had come another sound, that had struck alarmingly right through the very ground where they huddled. A few feet away, Grandfather Willow was groaning. The groan seemed to begin at his roots and work its way up his trunk. It was a most peculiar sound, one that Mrs Blackbird had never heard before. Grandfather Willow's old trunk was standing firm against the gale, but it was being terribly, oh so terribly battered! It was as if his poor roots were being torn right through as he tried to stand upright. Mrs Blackbird squeaked in fright and fluttered her wings against her husband.

"What is the matter, Mrs B?" grumbled he, as he stirred from the lethargy of the cold and dark.

But Mrs Blackbird had no chance to answer, for just then the terrible wind blew with all the strength it could muster, and that was terrible indeed, because the north wind had joined forces with the wild west wind from the Atlantic Ocean, and never such a blast had been endured in the garden before. From Grandfather Willow came a groan that was a very rendering of his whole trunk. The little Sweet William, its petals closed in terror, screamed high on the air, a sound that sent Mrs Blackbird into a dreadful panic; a rattle of alarm escaped her and then all she could do was fly, fly, fly in the wind to escape the tragedy that was happening all around.

For Grandfather Willow, bizarrely and awfully, was leaning across the gardener's washing line, which had broken with his weight, and his lower limbs had come to rest on the washing basket stone, where he had so often embraced the gardener children as they played on it and called it their pirate stone. Grandfather Willow, the mightiest and oldest tree in the garden, was face down on the ground!

The wind blew Mrs Blackbird right round Snail Corner and into the sturdy arms of the Escallonia where he stood at his post by the gate in the morning garden. Mrs Blackbird always called him, "Sir Escallonia Topknot" because of the high stem that protruded from his verify centre, where she often wished she dared perch. She gasped out her tale, her eyes rolling in terror. It seemed to her that the bad wind laughed as she told her story, and threw itself around the whole garden as if showing off its power. It seemed a long time before Sir Escallonia Topknot could bring himself to address her.

"The sound reached me also," he said at length, "I could not believe what I heard. But it is true."

Mrs Blackbird twittered pathetically. She did not even know if her husband was safe. Being a bird, she could not cry, but she wished at that moment that she were the gardener, who could, and who also could hide in the wooden house, safe from the death of trees.

"I am afraid!" she cried, "Oh, Sir, are you not afraid?"

Sir Escallonia Topknot wrapped his sturdy foliage around the blackbird to save her from being blown away in her distress.

"I am a Hedge," he announced, magnificently, "and although the wind may burn my leaves and blunt my edges, it will not blow me down as it does a tree. Our dear Grandfather Willow has paid the price of majesty."

"Oh," sobbed the blackbird, "How I wish I understood these things."

"Better be glad you don't," called the ubiquitous bramble, who had been listening from his shed wall, "and I should stay in this part of the garden tonight, if I were you. There is nothing you can do for the willow now. He's had it."

Mrs Blackbird thought privately that morning might never come to the garden again, but she said nothing. She huddled amongst the low trunks of the Escallonia, and wished Mr Blackbird were with her, for all his grumps. Indeed, she began to forget that he was at all gloomy or dull; it was comforting to think that he was always the same. She was quite sure, now she came to think of it, that when morning did come she would find him in exactly the same place where she had left him. She gave a small chirrup of pleasure as she thought of what he would say when he heard of her adventure:

"At least one of us had sense enough to stay put," he would remark, catching her eye with his bright glare, and then they would both look for worms in the soft earth that the rain had made, and eat them together. . . at length she slept, with only occasional little hiccoughs of fright when the wind gusted viciously round Snail Corner into the scorched bramble bush.

The measured tones of Sir Escallonia Topknot broke into her dreams.

"It is morning now, although the world is in gloom."

She blinked, as memory returned. Indeed it was a strange way to greet the day. The world was exhausted; devastation had entered where the garden had previously held fast. The grey day lifted a heavy head, without sound or delight.

"The wind has blown itself out, as the gardener would say," continued the Escallonia," although it seems to me that it has merely taken its murderous breath elsewhere. You must go, as I cannot, to pay our respects to Grandfather Willow; it is possible that he can still hear you, as some of his roots may be still in the earth. Go at once, and bring me back the news."

Mrs Blackbird, in a stupor of confusion, obeyed. She flew up in a flurry, round into the south garden, where the willow lay across the washing basket stone, his broken roots bare and tilted up to the sky. The sight was too awful; Mrs Blackbird felt the shock of it paralyse her very wings. She could not bear it; with her sharp eyes she searched for her husband. Contrary to her expectation, he was not in the place under the fuchsia where they had taken refuge the night before. The fuchsia, who had spent the night weeping, waved her soft trailing branches towards the willow tree. Mrs Blackbird edged her way close to the trunk, which lay completely horizontal; surely the world had tipped over in the night! But no, the other trees still stood all around, paying silent homage. But Grandfather Willow was no more.

In the crook of his trunk nestled a cluster of bright green leaves also uprooted, and also moribund. They were the leaves of the Sweet William she had admired the day before. Mrs Blackbird looked eagerly for the red-and-cream blossom, but of her there was no sign. It was as if the wind had ripped her out of all being; as if she had never existed at all in her brief glory. Mrs Blackbird hopped sadly down from the cluster of leaves, her head cocked to one side, as was her habit when contemplating the mysteries of life.

"There you are!" broke out a voice that was only very slightly grumpy. "I've been looking for you everywhere. Have you got any breakfast?"

Mrs Blackbird chirruped, squeaked and flurried all at once and hopped onto the trunk again. She did not remember that she had never been gladder to see her husband than at this moment; she was just glad to see him, as blackbirds are, because they are sociable birds and take a particular interest in the world and its doings.

"I've been looking at this tree," continued Mr Blackbird, "and it seems to me there are a lot of possibilities here for all sorts of things." He prowled round Grandfather Willow's boughs, casting a furtive glance at his wife every now and again. "He wanted to converse with me, you know. With me!" and his chest swelled out importantly. "I was a bit . . . taken up with other things at the time, ahem, you know . . . but it strikes me now that these boughs would make splendid homes – palatial residences, as it were, yes, indeed, for insects, grubs, nice new plants that will grow in the spring. There'll be lots of food, enormous quantities I should think, and just look at the earth that has been exposed round those roots, it will be just stuffed – just stuffed with earthworms! . . ." Mrs Blackbird thought she had never seen him so excited.

"Forgive him, sir," she muttered softly to Grandfather Willow, "He doesn't mean to be disrespectful."

And it seemed to her that the topmost branches of the tree, which were touching the flower bed under the bay window where the purple and orange crocuses would soon be showing their green tips, rustled a little as if to say,

"Leave him alone, leave him be."

On Sir Escallonia Topknot's instructions Mrs Blackbird flew round the garden carrying her important news to any plant, bush, tree or moving creature still not in the know, and Mr Blackbird followed behind her gobbling up any insect not quick enough to get out of his way. As the weeks passed and the winter days, in their turn, died away, the crocuses did indeed point their fresh leaves through the topmost branches of the old willow tree, for the Gardener did not move the trunk for a very long time. She did not sit beside it and weep, as Mrs Blackbird thought she might, for she had loved the tree almost beyond all the others, except of course for the little oak tree. The gardener children played on Grandfather Willow's trunk all the rest of the winter, and he joined in their pirate game much more than ever before, because he was now their pirate ship, along which they ran and called excitedly, "Swab the decks, cabin-boy! Land ahoy!"

In the spring, when the garden was once again the sunlit garden, the old willow tree had a surprise in store for them. All along the length of the old trunk sprouted new little twigs bearing bright buds, then tiny yellow leaves that caught the sun against the fresh green of the lawn. The gardener smiled and said that she would really have to plant the new trees somewhere else, or Grandfather Willow would soon be catching her washing again just the way he used to. And as the wind blew at last from the warm south the old trunk would sometimes give the faintest of creaks, almost imperceptible, but plainly audible to Mrs

Blackbird. It seemed to her then as if the old tree was laughing, although she couldn't be sure.

Mrs Blackbird, looking at her own new babies snug in the nest made from Grandfather Willow's twigs and his cosy leaves, gave a sharp little trill of joy. She thought that, perhaps, in the depths of his trunk, the old tree would still hear.

16. A Coming to Earth

The summer came, and went, and Mrs Blackbird's babies were quite grown up. The winter that followed the rending of Grandfather Willow was filled with a multiplication of storms. They were so many and so furious that the unremarkable osiers, who had very shallow roots, were thrown almost out of the ground. The gardener looked very serious as she contemplated them.

"They will have to come out," she declared, to no-one in particular, but everyone was listening. "We will have to prepare ourselves for more change."

She discussed the matter with one of the gardener children, who liked Maths and could do many clever sums in his head. They were sitting on the doorstep in the morning garden, on a day in early spring, where the sun had just risen over Sir Escallonia Topknot's foremost twig.

"This is The Four Times' Table Garden," announced the gardener child, solemnly, "because last summer we planted peas four times and the snails came and ate them every time."

"That's true," agreed the gardener, "and I had four attempts at planting the Escallonia before he reached his present state of glory. The wind and the salt from the sea got him every time. But just look how sturdy he is now!"

The gardener child was wholly taken up with his new idea.

"Look at those little sticks!" he cried. (He meant the tiny new redcurrant bushes that the gardener had stuck into the ground as twigs, despairing of the shy redcurrant's ability ever to produce worthwhile fruit). "There are eight of them! Two times four!"

"And sixteen snails already!" said the gardener, but she was just teasing. The clever son had bought her some copper wire, and she hoped to erect defences around her plants this year. She would also plant garlic, which would help to keep snails away. The last resort would be a trap for the them, so that they could be sent away to a restaurant in Spain and gobbled up as they gobbled her garden. . . and so the gardener planned, while the child ran around finding new sums.

The next-door shed had had great holes torn out of it by the gale and was now patched up with different shapes of unpainted board.

When the shed had been repaired, the ubiquitous bramble had suffered a great deal of damage, being trampled on and stamped out of the way. But the gardener child was enjoying finding the new shapes on the shed – three long rectangles together, a square, but no circles! . . . and the gardener got up and walked around, planning.

As well as being windy, the winter had been very wet. New drains would be required. Grandfather Willow was no longer there to take up

113

the excess water with his roots, so nothing would grow under her bedroom window until some sort of drainage was put in. The garden was covered in wet leaves and old brown stalks, which she had not cleared up because she had lost her composting area entirely. This was because the Lady of the Lamplit Wood had given her not one cherry tree, but two, and the only place for the one-times-two tree to go was where the garden waste had been thrown. In planting the second cherry tree the gardener had dug up lots of rubbish; broken glass, concrete and slate that had lain for many years beneath the garden waste . . . and so it went on. She picked up a slate that had blown off the roof in the last gale. This had been the gale that had torn up the osiers. The man who watched the distant hills said that the wind had reached one hundred and twelve miles an hour.

"There's a figure for you," said the gardener to the mathematical child, and stuck her woolly hat on his head, for it was a very early spring day and still cold.

"A sixty-one-year-old hat fits me!" he exclaimed, and the gardener laughed.

She worked hard at the thick red roots of the unremarkable osiers, until her back ached. She had bought a new tree to go just there, and it would have to go into the earth soon, or it would die.

"I must get some compost," though the gardener, and then thought, "I must *make* some compost!"

And so brand new compost bins were ordered, and some pallets arranged to make a place for all the twigs and sticks that would take longer to turn into compost, and the gardener began to feel more cheerful. Mr and Mrs Blackbird were already very busy in the exciting new area uncovered by the osiers' uprooting; by the gate, where the old rose root had been and where the two million dandelions would come, the snowdrop held her pretty head delicately against the rich black earth; and all over the garden, now that she had cleared the rotting stems of mombresia, flourished bright green stems of daffodils, soon to be gold in the garden.

The garden, however, was united in disapproval.

"It will mean men with machines," growled the splendid Oleria. They will dig everything up for their drainage, you'll see."

"We are so small. They will stamp over us!" whispered the crocuses.

"There will be no willows at all to shield me," mourned The Lady Fuchsia.

"Will she think I too should be cut down?" worried the sad oak tree.

"Might she notice me at last?" murmured a tree whose voice had never been heard in the garden. It was shrouded by the spreading hazel, and even the gardener did not remember that it was there.

When the new tree came to live where the unremarkable osiers had lived, she was small and slender, but quite, quite remarkable. She had a voice, which they all heard, minutes after her roots had snuggled down into their new bed. Her voice was of velvet, and her vowels wonderfully elongated.

"I am Victoria Plum!" she sang, "*Prunus Domestica*, don't you know?"

Silence.

"I say! I say, everyone! Didn't you hear me? Don't you want to know who I am and where I come from? The best, the very best, nursery, don't you know . . . "

The Oleria coughed, coldly and disapprovingly. No one else replied.

Poke, poke! The Rosa Rugosa shoved her longest spray through the south fence.

"They won't answer, you know! They don't want you. Too many changes, too many changes! And the horse has never come back, no, never! And won't! And won't!"

The plum tree did not know what she meant by the horse, but she got the message, loud and clear, that no one would welcome her or talk to her. She drooped her lovely stem, and did not try to talk again to the garden. If her voice was heard, it was quietly, in song, to herself.

"She is of a different tradition," muttered the Sweet William, who were Jacobites to a man, "She comes from enemy country. She does not belong here. Go back, go back!" they called crossly, but Victoria Plum closed her ears to them and listened instead to where the littlest gardener child was playing, at the top end of the garden, on the seesaw that the clever son had made.

"See-saw, Margery Daw," the child sang, "Johnny shall have a new master; and he shall have but a penny a day, because he won't work any faster . . ."

Now there was a song from her own country! That was better! And from then on that was the song she chose to sing, when the loneliness of her new home was too much.

"Margery Daw!" jeered the cheeky privet, "That's a good name for you. Try saying that with a plum in your mouth!" And he laughed so hard at his own joke that his tiniest twigs shook.

"Come on, Madge!" shouted the bramble, who was doing his best to be ubiquitous again, "Give us an old knees-up Maggie Daw!"

"What about a Scraggy-Daw?" guffawed the privet, although this was pathetically *un*funny, and no one else laughed.

And so they ragged the Victoria Plum until she stopped singing at all. And then there were two silent trees in the garden, the hidden one who had never been noticed, and the new one who would never grow tall and bonny where she was not wanted.

Things in the garden had come to a pretty pass.

"But where is The Silver Witch?" asked the shy redcurrant, of her friend the blackcurrant.

"She does not come here any more," sighed the blackcurrant. "Meanness and destruction hold sway."

There was a loud snort from Sir Escallonia Topknot.

"Get a grip, you thornless wonders!" he boomed. The Silver Witch has left us for good. She cannot stay for ever in a place such as this. The world is a big place, and full of things we cannot imagine."

The Victoria Plum dared to look up.

"I have seen something of the world," she whispered, "if you would like to hear tell."

Trees and plants rustled their way round to see and hear the temerity of the new tree. The Victoria Plum thought, "It is now or never!" and swung her long thin arms to the sky.

"In the land from which I came," she trilled, but softly still, the wind blows less, the sun shines more, and it is warm, bringing wonderful panoply of flowers and trees, of many domestic varieties and even some exotica. I have been told," and here she dropped her voice slightly, "that I will never bear fruit in this climate, but am here for my beauty and for the image I bring of a well-sheltered and fruitful land. Your gardener . . . your gardener has had her fill of the wild wind. I will make her think of gardens where the breeze is light, fat bees buzz in the flowers and in the autumn the soft fruit drops from the trees . . . even if . . .even if . . . I can never bear my own plums. I have a function," she looked round at them all, quite fiercely now, "a function, as a storyteller."

No one spoke, but they listened with all their new leaves.

"There is one more thing," said the Victoria Plum, a little more boldly now, "I know where your Silver Witch has gone."

"What do you mean?" asked the splendid Oleria sternly. "How can you know, you who are new, and foreign?"

"It is because I am foreign, and have kept silence," answered the Victoria Plum, that I heard and saw her pass, and you did not," (and some of the garden inhabitants had the grace to blush a little at the thought of their Silver Witch overhearing their jeering), "She has chosen a silent foreigner in which to live, for a time."

"You cannot mean yourself, I hope!" This was Sir Escallonia Topknot now, who hardly ever spoke sternly. The cheek of this newcomer! "Where is our Silver Witch?"

"There," nodded the Victoria Plum. And they followed her gaze to the tree who never spoke, and who had remained unnoticed in the garden since time immemorial. "She has taken up her abode in the tree that peoples the Steppes of Russia, that lives through snow and ice and the bitterest of winds; the Silver Birch."

When the gardener walked through her garden that spring, she looked first at the remains of Grandfather Willow. Lots of young willow stems were growing out of his trunk, in glorious, spiky disarray.

"Teenagers would pay a fortune for that hairstyle," she said, just as if he could hear her.

She stopped next at the sad oak tree.

"You have not been blown down like those unreliable willows," she remarked.

"Having his knees permanently crossed in terror probably helps," muttered the privet from his corner.

"Don't worry any more; we won't be cutting you down," said the gardener to the oak tree, and stroked his smooth young trunk.

The oak tree's neighbour was the spreading hazel, which the gardener had cut back a very little occasionally without really paying it much attention. The hazel tree did not bear fruit. But this time, something – who knew what? – moved her to remember that the spreading hazel was spreading around, and nearly enveloping, a small, slender, elegant tree with the most beautiful and delicate little pale-green leaves.

"My birch tree!" she exclaimed in great joy, "How could I forget you were there? I will cut back the hazel straight away, and then everyone will see and admire you. You bring the image and savour of the lands of ice and snow, where your great forests line the horizon from end to end! And you," she said, turning to the little but determined Victoria Plum, "will remind us of the blessings of warmth and our own country just across the sunlit sea. In my garden lives the whole world."

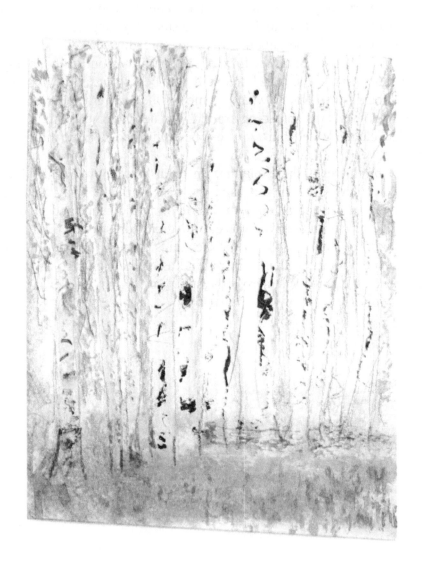

17. Foundlings

The first really remarkable day of spring was the day when, in the morning garden, three greenfinch appeared and sat on Sir Escallonia Topknot's topknot. They surveyed the scene, for all the world like three building surveyors in their smart green waistcoats, just as if they were considering building an extension or envisaging a quite different layout to the sunlit garden. Sir Escallonia Topknot rustled his leaves, the edges of which were quite curled over and browned by the beating wind; but the greenfinch did not move. They took their ease, staring hard at the fresh new green of the chives, and the tiny, pale green buds on the gooseberry bush and exchanging pertinent remarks with each other.

"Do they think they'll find babies under the gooseberry bush?" grizzled the bramble, who was often sarcastic. Now the finches knew that this story about babies under the gooseberry bush was what was

called "an old wives tale" and they twittered their amusement.

"When we lay our eggs there'll be plenty of babies! You'll see! You'll see!"

"We'll *hear*, more likely," grumped the bramble bush, "Noisy young fledglings!"

And Jack Sparrow, who not long ago had been a fledging himself, puffed out his chest and whistled as loudly as he could. The bramble bush pulled down its wide leaves hard over its ears, and muttered something about no more peace and quiet in the garden. The greenfinch flew off, right out of the garden, to survey other possible nesting places. But what next? There was Mrs Blackbird – Mrs Prim and Proper herself (as the bramble bush called her) and she had perched, not on the washing basket stone, as usual, but right on the top of the clothes line pole, and then, would you believe it, she hopped right onto the line itself and started swinging on it! Jack's eyes nearly popped out of his head.

"It's spring!" called the rowan tree, pushing out his pointed buds as fast as he could.

"We know!" called the daffodils that marched right across the top garden, like a school of ballerinas all decked out in gold.

"Wait for us!" cried the tête-à-tête daffodils at the foot of the south garden, "We're want to dance too!"

And the purple crocus smiled, because she had been looking out for quite some time and had braved many cold winds in order to greet this moment.

Out stepped the gardener. She paused on the step and breathed in the air, which was no longer harsh with cold but ever so slightly what you might call *balmy*. She sighed a little over Sir Escallonia

Topknot's frazzled twigs and gave the bramble bush a rather searching glance; but she seemed delighted with the straight young chives and promised them that she would bring the gardener children to taste them that very day.

Then she brought out the box. Everyone in the garden strained forward to look. What could be in it? All of them knew that boxes contained exciting things. And everyone was ready for a surprise. Could it be a new plant to join them? Where could it go? Of course, thought the bramble, that old southernwood bush has gone with winter's blast; she will put the new plant there, where it will be a companion to me in my old age."

"Hmm," said the gardener, as she passed the next door shed, where the old southernwood bush had been used to observe life, "I must put something there to hide all that patchwork of a repair job on that shed. But for now I need ... yes, there's the very thing!"

And she stopped in front of a great flourishing bunch of stems that later would bring the white hyacinths; and she took something out of the box that was not at all like a new plant. It was *roundish*, but not quite round (so the nearby potentilla observed) and it was *very* brightly coloured, all glittery and frivolous. "Just like me, really," thought the potentilla.

The gardener placed the roundish object right in the centre of the hyacinth stems.

"Oh!" cried they, in surprise, "Nothing like this has ever happened to us before!"

The gardener did not stop there. She looked very seriously at the sad oak tree, but he was always the last to produce his leaves, and his trunks were still too young and thin for her purposes. Aha! The rowan was better – older, and with more nooks and crannies (wrinkles, said the bramble bush, who was watching from his narrow space beside the next door shed). The gardener placed another of the roundish objects there.

"They're eggs!" screeched Jack Sparrow, "Just look, just look!"

And eggs they were. Four very large ones – the whitebeam tree counted them as they were hidden right up at the top of the garden, in amongst the golden daffodils and behind the cumbersome ash tree that *would* try and take over the little beech beside it. There were a dozen eggs that were about the size of goose eggs (so the Rosa Rugosa suggested, who had actually seen geese once in the field where she had spread beyond the garden) and there were eight small eggs that could have been greenfinch eggs had they not been wrapped in such rainbow colours, and, as everyone knows, greenfinch eggs are not rainbow-coloured but a sort of dull creamy colour with only a few little black flecks.

"Are there fledglings in the eggs?" asked Jack, of no one in particular.

Everyone looked not at the bramble bush, whose opinions were sometimes mistrusted, but at Sir Escallonia Topknot, who was very wise and knowledgeable, because he could see right over the next door waste ground right down to the sunlit sea.

"There is a ship," said Sir Escallonia Topknot finally, "which at present is striding the horizon like a great star fallen from the skies. It cannot swim; yet it does not sink. The world has many things in it that we cannot know, and therefore do not understand. "My opinion," and here he bent his topmost twigs down low, and the chives beneath trembled with excitement, "my opinion is that these eggs, as you call them, are not eggs at all, unless a chick of some sort should emerge. What they *are*, of course, is another matter entirely; and that, we shall soon discover, for here come the gardener children, and they will surely know."

"It's Easter!" cried the gardener children, in just the same way that the garden had called, "It's spring!"

"The Easter Egg Hunt!" they called, and ran about the garden finding and counting and putting all the glittering eggs back into the box from which the gardener had taken them in the first place.

"I've found one!" they would each yell as yet another branch of rowan or hyacinth clump would yield up a shiny egg.

"Look here! This way!" Jack Sparrow chirped, when he was the first to find another egg.

"Look at me!" called the potentilla, "I have one! I'm hiding one!"

"This is fun," said the sad oak tree, "even if I don't have one."

"Ouch!" cried the gardener, as a poky twig caught her in the eye, "My contact lens! That willow twig has poked it out! Don't anyone stand on it!"

Aghast, the willow tree dropped its head. So did all the gardener children, as they crawled carefully round the place where the tiny piece of plastic had fallen. They looked and looked. Jack Sparrow looked too, but even he couldn't find it . . . until, there! It lay glistening, right in the very heart of the purple crocus! She was keeping it safe. Jack hopped immediately under the crocus's head, which normally drooped, but which she was now holding up as high as she could so that the precious lens did not fall.

"Here it is! Here it is!" he chirped, and the oldest gardener child, who was very good at listening and watching, saw him, and the crocus, and on her deeply blushing petal the lens gleaming in the sun.

"The sparrow found it!" called the child, and happiness flew down on the garden again.

"Look!" cried the potentilla, who in her amazement had forgotten that she was frivolous and flirtatious,   "They are eating the eggs!"

And so they were. The eggs did not have chicks in them, but were hollow and made of something that appeared to be extremely delicious.

"But why . . .?" began the potentilla.

"Ssshhh!" hissed everyone, for the gardener was explaining.

"The eggs make us think of the stone that rolled away from Jesus' tomb on the first Easter Day," the gardener said.

"They make *me* think of baby chicks," said one of the gardener children, "and what a racket the birds were making in our garden this morning! They kept flying in and out, tweet, tweet, tweet . . . "

"Making nests for their eggs," smiled the gardener.

"Is an egg like a stone?" wondered the potentilla, and looked in puzzlement at the stones lying round about her roots. "A stone is not alive," she thought, "it does not breathe, or feel. What use is a stone?"

And it was true that the whole garden was bursting with new life; buds and little curly leaves, tall stems and twigs vigorous enough to knock out the gardener's contact lens. Everywhere you looked there were new colours and new flowers, and birds breaking out in song. Only the stones were just stones, perfectly still and dull.

After the gardener and the children had gone into the wooden house and the fun and noise had stopped, the potentilla found herself thinking about the stones at her roots. She kept a close eye on them in case they suddenly did something surprising.

The stones were just stones. But as the potentilla nodded her budding stems downwards, she noticed Jack Sparrow who was pecking about. During the search for the contact lens one of the stones had been moved; and underneath it was a fascinating new world for Jack, full of grubs and tiny insects, all scurrying trying to find a new place to hide and lay *their* eggs. Jack was having a great time poking around in there . It was dry and cosy under the stone. As the potentilla looked at the new world that Jack had discovered she remembered too how during the winter the rainwater had run away from her roots, round the stone and down towards the bottom of the garden. She thought about how the thrush would use the stone to tap a snail's shell, and how this helped the gardener, because after the thrush had tapped them on the stone there were fewer snails to eat the plants she tried to grow. And when the potentilla told the crocus all these things the oak tree listened, and told the potentilla that really she was not frivolous at all, because she had discovered a truth about stones, and wasn't the garden made of stone underneath its rich brown earth?

On the ground by the stone lay a tiny piece of something rich and brown that had fallen from one of the brightly wrapped eggs.

"Oho!" cried Jack as his bright gaze fell on it, "Now I shall find out what the eggs are made of!" And he gobbled up the tiny rich brown thing as fast as he could.

"Beugghhh!" he spat it back out again, and pretended to be sick, as teenagers do. "They can keep their eggs that are not eggs," he twittered to anyone who was listening, "Give me a nice fat grub any day. Now where was that stone that was rolled away . . .? It's the best bit of the whole garden."

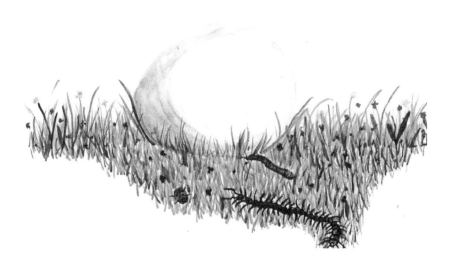

Lightning Source UK Ltd.
Milton Keynes UK
UKOW06f2131140616

276265UK00009B/34/P